D1554205

# The Beckoning Spark

# The Puzzle Box Chronicles: Book 6

# The Beckoning Spark

Shawn P. McCarthy

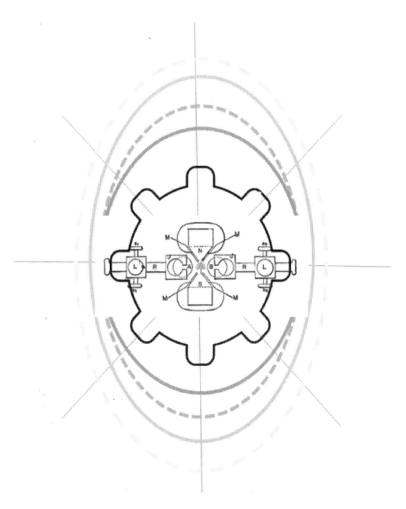

*The Puzzle Box Chronicles*
*Book 6*

Book cover design by Teodora Chinde
Printed in the United States of America
First Printing, 2021
ISBN-13: 978-0-9968967-9-5 (Dark Spark Press)
ISBN- 10: 0-9968967-9-1

**Dark Spark Press**

www.DarkSparkPress.com

Publisher.DarkSparkPress@gmail.com

# Chapter 1

## *Tentative Steps*

Bruised. Battered. Wet.

But somehow still alive.

Amanda inhales deeply, crawls across pebbles, and pulls herself up to the top of a riverbank. She starts to stand but her soaked dress clings to her legs. The first step causes her to stumble.

Hands land hard against stones. She cries out, but there is no one to hear.

So, she rolls over and tries to gather her thoughts. There are clouds above, but they seem less dark now. The storm is dissipating. Is she finally safe?

She tries to remember.

Amanda… Grant. Yes, that's her name. She knows that. Then she starts to recall random moments from the last half hour. The memories are jolting. But they also bring a prideful smile.

She remembers an apocalyptic level of rain.

Then, to avoid the two men who pursued her, she leapt into a flooded and raging Mississippi River. The storm caused the river waters to move much faster and wilder than she expected. During her crossing, she collided with, and was nearly swallowed by, a massive, uprooted elm tree carried downstream by the furious waters.

And there, entangled in the elm's branches, she saw sweeping destruction. Death. Terrible things. The tree carried her to the point where she became hopelessly lost. When she managed to break free and kick her way toward the Illinois shore, she was out of energy. Barely conscious.

So that must be where she is now. East side of the river. God knows where.

Then Amanda remembers something else, which might explain why this place seems so isolated. She recalls being pushed far off course by the high water. The current forced her into a part of the river that had spilled its banks and rushed out over a massive flood plain. The flood had cut a muddy channel and the waters pushed her there, deep into the unknown.

Then she remembers one more thing. The recollection makes her sit up with a start.

Right before she fell into exhausted sleep, she saw something incongruous. Both the grass and the trees of a nearby field looked strangely white. There was a path at the far side that led into the woods, and the edges of the path looked blood-red in color.

Wincing in pain, Amanda stumbles to her feet, determined to investigate the white landscape. She turns in that direction, but everything looks different now. She takes a few steps. Rubs her eyes. Eventually she realizes why she saw those hues. The trees and their leaves must have been covered with droplets. Storm water still lingering on the branches. In her exhausted state, the reflecting light must have looked bright white to her. And the opening that looked red? Just a few maple trees at the edge of the woods starting to change to their autumn colors.

That's all it was. A trick of the light.

Her head hurts. Bumps and bruises distract. She can't think clearly. Amanda steels herself and scans the field, looking for the tattered sign she saw.

And there it is, beside the trail, marking the red-leaf entrance to the woods. Fading letters read *Welcome to Angel Falls*.

The words stir a memory. What did she hear that crewman say when she was stowing away on The Delta Lady?

"Stay north of Angel Falls."

But why?

It's too late to worry. She's already here. Behind her, there's only mud and river. To either side, there's dense forest. Her only clear path is forward, past the old sign, the red leaves, and then on to wherever the path leads.

The decrepit dome she saw from the river must hint at civilization. She will head there. If she finds a town, there are a few things she very much wants to do. The first is to take a bath. Second is to get something to eat. Third is to send a telegram.

Amanda is quite done with running away. She is done with sneaking aboard trains and boats and hiding from people. That means she must find a way to buy her own train ticket. She has no money, but she knows she will find a way.

The final thing she wants to do is to buy a small notebook. After spending the past few weeks reading the journal of Victor Marius, she thinks it's time to start some kind of diary of her own.

# Chapter 2

## *From a General Store*

The detached barn door beneath Jeb Thomas' feet provides him with a steady ride. It spins slowly as it moves downriver, giving him a constantly changing view. He drifts along on his makeshift raft with no particular urgency. He spends the time scanning the banks for any sign of Amanda. He also keeps an eye out for anything that looks like a town. Spire of a church? Smokestack? Anything that might lead him back to civilization.

When he spots a hint of coal smoke in the distance, he grabs the flat board he's been using as a rudder and thrusts it into the water. Holding it at an angle, he steers his raft toward the eastern shore, landing with a hard thud on the Illinois side of the river. The water pressure behind him pushes the barn door a few feet up the bank, and Jeb finds it amusing to just step off. He crossed the mighty Mississippi during a major flood and barely got his shoes wet.

A fifteen-minute walk brings him to the outskirts of a small town. Jeb sees no evidence of Amanda along the way. He has no interest in the town's name. All he cares is whether he can send a telegraph. He spots some wires and follows them through the village. They end at a general store.

Inside, he passes by racks of food and dry goods. Near the back, he finds a desk with a telegraph key. There's only one clerk in the building. Jeb paces impatiently while the man cuts and wraps a chicken. Eventually the shopkeeper comes to the desk and dons his black visor.

"I need to send several telegrams," says Jeb. "And when we're done, I need you to point me to a place where I can find transportation."

"Yep. Can do. But you know there ain't no train here. The 5:30 coach can take you about 10 miles to the closest station."

"That's fine."

The clerk nods and picks up his pencil.

Jeb's first telegram is sent to one of his East Coast union associates. Jeb informs him he's heading back to Boston and asks for any leads he may have for employment—contract negotiations, coordinating meetings, anything at all.

The second telegram goes to San Francisco. He tells his contact at the pier there's been a change of plans. He won't be visiting the West Coast anytime soon. They need to find themselves a different union coordinator.

Jeb then gives careful thought to his third message.

He's reluctantly accepted he's lost Amanda's trail again. His dreams of rescuing her and winning her back have been deferred. But he won't give up on finding her. That also would mean giving up any chance to find out what's inside of the puzzle box she's stashed somewhere back in Boston. He has a hunch that's where she's headed – back there. To claim it.

Maybe he can recruit Devlin Richards to help find both the box and the girl. He slowly dictates his message.

"Can you read that back?" Jeb asks the clerk. The man adjusts his visor and calls out the text.

RETURNING TO BOSTON WITHIN THE WEEK [STOP]
GIRL MAY BE HEADING THERE TOO. [STOP] SHE REMAINS OUR BEST LEAD FOR FINDING THE BOX. [STOP] KEEP AN EYE OUT FOR HER AND I'LL HELP MAKE PLANS WHEN I ARRIVE IN A FEW DAYS. [STOP]

He pays the clerk and gets directions to where the stagecoach stops.

"Usually," the clerk says, "that ride can make it to the station just in time for you to catch the 7:36 train to Cincinnati."

Jeb thanks him and mutters "good to know."

# Chapter 3

## *Angel Falls*

Amanda heads toward the red leaves that mark the start of the path. The trail leads into the woods. She finds it overgrown and neglected, but she's able to make her way through.

She hopes to spot the vaulted rooftop again. As she picks her way through the overgrowth, she realizes just how lost she must be. When she reaches the top of a knoll, she finds a break in the trees. But she sees no houses. No church steeples. No factories or stores. She sees nothing but fields and trees.

The dome is nowhere to be found.

Another half mile. And there, finally, there is something. She sees the tip of a spire directly ahead and recognizes it as a decorative lightning rod, perched atop the crest of a building.

She presses on. A whitetail deer crosses the path, notices her, and bounds away. From the time of day and position of the sun, Amanda knows she's walking southeast. She believes that's the general direction of the tri-state border where Indiana, Kentucky, and Illinois all meet.

What she really hopes to find is a church. Maybe she could appeal to a pastor's sense of charity. Beg a meal. Maybe get a few coins to help send her telegram and buy her notebook.

Eventually she emerges from the woods, and what she sees stops her cold. She rubs her eyes. But the view is quite real. In the big clearing sits an immense house made almost entirely of stone, iron, and glass.

She has found the dome. It's the top of this home. The dome includes glass panes shaped in alternating diamonds and squares. It looks a bit like a greenhouse, but more majestic and dripping with wrought-iron trim. Perhaps this is some type of institution? Maybe a monastery or a sanatorium? There is a slight smell of sulfur in the air. Maybe it's a health facility built over mineral waters.

For a moment, Amanda just stares.

She notices an addition on the back of the main building. That part vaguely resembles a small cathedral. Some of its windows are broken, and part of the roof has collapsed. Despite the condition, its interior lights have been lit, and on this cloudy afternoon, it literally glows.

The path she's been following curves toward the front of the glass house. As she views the building from different angles, she forms another idea about its purpose. Perhaps it's an ornate conservatory. But the interior space does not seem to hold plants and flowers. It's more open.

She hesitates before knocking on the door. She can see deep inside now and spies a grand room containing several large, brightly colored spheres. They hang at odd levels.

Then, for the first time, she sees human beings. But they're not inside the home. They are outside in the yard. Maybe they've been there all along. She's not sure why she didn't notice them.

Some of the people follow walkways, looking very purposeful in their activities. Others appear lost and aimless. Some carry crates and sacks between the house and a nearby barn. Some just stand motionless. She sees one man crawling on all fours like an animal, grunting and wheezing. Amanda backs away.

To her left, there is a nearly naked woman, mumbling and walking in circles. Beyond that, a man in rags lays face-up in the mud, groaning and running his hands over his face. At first, she assumes these people are other survivors of the flood. Then she decides they are here because of other circumstances.

Some have old clothes and hairstyles that have not been popular for decades.

Nervously, she puts some distance between herself and the others, moving toward the cover of a large rhododendron near the front portico.

It takes her some time to comprehend what she's seeing. It's not all madness. There's a rough order in place. The ones who look lost and confused are but a few. Mostly she sees men and women standing in a line near the barn. They form an orderly queue and look straight ahead, arms at their sides.

Amanda longs to talk to someone. She wants to ask questions, or maybe get directions. But she's scared. This all seems so… uncertain.

Two dapper men exit the barn. They look like bankers or lawyers, but more unkempt – with hair askew and ties pulled loose. Their shirttails hang out beneath dusty coats.

One of the men carries an extra suit of clothes. While walking, he attempts to fold the jacket, pants, and shirt, but they look damaged and messy.

They head in her direction, and she realizes they're walking toward a wagon parked near the front door. Amanda hadn't noticed the wagon until now either. She rubs her temples and finds her hair smeared with blood and mud.

"Are you just going to leave him like that?" One man asks the other.

"Hell yes. You think he deserves anything more?"

"No," the first man replies. "I guess he does not. But I must say I'm not at all sure what we were dealing with in there. It's most troubling."

"That's not our concern. I got the suit back. Someone will be sent to deal with him, and I suppose he'll be removed. Mrs. Lethe will see to that. For all I care, he can damn well stay right where he is, naked and bleeding, until she decides."

The man places the folded suit on the bed of a wagon. Amanda can see the coat and pants are even dirtier than the suits the men are wearing. She also smells something – like a mix of sulfur and pig excrement.

"Who would ever want to come deal with the likes of him anyway? Looking like he does. Smelling like he does."

"My guess is she'll pay someone. Or recruit someone. Then he becomes their problem, eh?"

Both of the men chuckle. Then they notice Amanda.

"Goodness gracious, child, who are you?" one asks.

"What on earth are you doing here?" demands the other.

Amanda shyly bids them hello, uncertain whether she's been caught trespassing. The men approach, not with anger, but with a genuine concern. In her bone-thin state, with ripped dress and smears of dirt, she must look like a refugee from a distant war.

"I… I'm sorry to just show up here," she stammers. "I mean no harm. It's just … I'm lost."

12

The men look at each other. "Every time there's a huge rain," one says. They both nod. Then they laugh.

"Well," says one, "it's been quite some time since we've had someone new who washed in."

They extend their hands. "Why don't you tell us what happened?"

Amanda confides in them about being chased, crossing the river, and getting pushed far downstream. Then she tells them about going off course, through a break in the dike, with the high water pushing her beyond the usual course of the river. She describes pulling herself up the bank, through the rocks and mud, then wandering through the countryside. She describes how she spotted the dome and made her way toward it.

"What in the world is this place?" she asks. She can hear the sense of wonder in her own voice.

"Quite a sight, isn't it?" The men then exchange looks, then nod. It seems they are agreeing it's okay to tell Amanda a little more.

"It was built by Sir Abraham Elohim. He came from overseas. Made his fortune upriver. Investor mostly. Builder. This became his summer home decades ago. Apparently, he wanted something big and open. Bright and different. But he also wanted it to seem like it was part of its surroundings."

"It's certainly all of those things," Amanda says, "especially with the vines growing on the sides. Does Sir Elohim still live here?"

"Oh. Well, that's a bit of an open question. He is seen occasionally. By some. But his wife, Mrs. Lethe, she never liked the city, so she lives here always. It's just her and her servants. Many years now."

"Does that mean the two of you don't live here?"

They both laugh. And again, they look at each other. But when they realize she's serious, one of them responds "I suppose… we are guests."

"Yes. That's right. Guests," says the other. "Long-term guests. But still…"

Amanda wants very much to get out of her filthy and damp clothes. But she's compelled to learn more. "How did you end up here?"

"In my case, I needed to straighten out a bit of business."

"Yes, me too," says the other. "That's an excellent way to put it."

Amanda realizes they don't want to share too much. She decides to stop asking for their details and instead plays on their sympathies. "Could one of you, possibly, give me a ride into town?"

They both frown. "What town?"

"Any town is many miles from here."

"And there's no easy way to get there."

"No. No real road at all," says the younger of the two men. "Though I do hope to go in that direction myself too. Maybe sometime soon."

"Tomorrow?" she asks.

He laughs at her persistence. "I suppose tomorrow would be quite a fine time, if that can be arranged. The decision isn't mine though. But if we do manage to make the trip sometime soon, and if you are able to ride along, then yes! I'd absolutely welcome the company."

She finds the wording strange, but withholds comment.

"What's your name?" the older man inquires.

"Amanda," she says, offering her hand. "Amanda Grant."

They introduce themselves as Raymond Crowley and Edward Purling. Compared to the other men she's met in her recent travels, they seem far more eloquent and polished, in spite of the rumpled look of their clothes. Maybe she was right about them being bankers or lawyers.

"Country gentlemen," says Raymond. It's as if he read her thoughts. "That's what we like to call ourselves. The gentlemen part is a bit tenuous though."

"And we are quite charmed to meet you, my dear," says Edward. "As you can imagine, visitors are rare here, and often when we do get visitors they are lost."

"Where is *here*, exactly?"

"Well, let me first ask which way you came in!"

Amanda is perplexed.

"Listen," Edward continues. "We will have time to chat. But for now, why don't we take you into the house and introduce you to Mrs. Lethe?"

"Thank you. I'd like that. So, I guess her name isn't Mrs. Elohim, like her husband?"

They ignore the question. "You look like you could use a good meal. Her kitchen staff usually keeps lunch warm, sometimes all the way until dinner."

"I... I don't want to impose."

"Nonsense," Raymond says. He takes her hand. "She's quite welcoming. The fostering type. She'll be glad to have a visitor."

As they approach the house, Amanda notes the top part of the mammoth front doors include a stretch of leaded glass, etched and beveled at each edge. The panes create a complex spiral, and the center of the spiral is filled with colored circles.

As they pass through the door, Amanda is spellbound by what she sees.

The room is immense. The colored orbs she spotted through the windows turn out to be metal. Each one is painted to look like a planet of the solar system. They hang from fat ceiling beams and are illuminated by gas lights. The smallest—apparently Mercury—is yellowish-white and looks to be about 24 inches in diameter. The largest, Jupiter, with bands of red and beige, is at least nine feet across. It hangs near the highest point of the arched ceiling.

"Sir Elohim was a bit of an astronomer," Raymond explains. "He built these models specifically to hang over his work area. Said it helped him monitor their orbits. Look up there. See? They actually move!"

Amanda realizes the orbs don't hang directly from the beams. They hang from an elaborate track and chain system attached to the beams. The rig lets the planets slowly rotate and orbit, apparently at varying speeds, around a crystal-like ball that hangs directly below the midpoint of the dome.

"But," Edward adds, "the movement is quite slow, day in and day out. Quite remarkable, really."

They stop beneath the metallic orb that's painted like Earth.

A maid walks out to greet them. "Hello, gentlemen. I thought you had departed."

"We were preparing to leave, but we found this young woman wandering outside. She's quite lost, poor thing. We thought maybe you could give her something to eat?"

The housekeeper looks Amanda up and down, then starts to laugh. "My goodness, aren't you a sight? Oh, how many months has it been since we've had a visitor?" She smiles sympathetically. "Yes, of course, we can help. Let's head down the hall, and we'll set you up with... well, we'll find something."

Amanda breathes a sigh of relief.

They traverse a marble-tiled passage and Amanda catches glimpses through the open doors. She sees a huge structure on one side and decides that must be the church-like addition she saw from the outside. From the inside, that part of the house looks as decrepit as the exterior. Part of a wall has caved in, and water runs through the opening. It creates an interior stream that spills across the floor, feeding a line of moss at its edge.

The maid sees Amanda staring.

"Fascinating, isn't it? That used to be the home's main salon. They held many balls there. Grand gatherings. But when heavy rains come, a nearby creek often fills up and overflows. When that happens, the water washes right through there. You can see it now, still draining from the recent storm. It was poor planning to build here, really. The floods eventually undermined that part of the foundation."

Amanda looks at the invading vegetation. "So, when it started spilling into here – that must have started happening some years ago?"

"Yes," the housekeeper responds. "Some time ago indeed."

Raymond interrupts. "Is Mrs. Lethe still present? It would be wonderful if Amanda could meet the lady of the house."

The maid shakes her head. "I'm afraid that isn't a good idea right now. Madam is not in the best of spirits." She leans forward, whispering, "You know, what with the other visitor. The one you helped trap in the barn."

The two men nod. "We understand perfectly."

"By the way, did you manage to get your suit back?" the maid inquires.

"Yes, yes. We took it from him. It's not in good shape, I'm afraid."

"Please understand that Madam is terribly sorry. She's promised to pay you for another one."

"Nonsense. I think we can clean it. And if we can't, well, I'll come to see her then."

The housekeeper thanks them.

Raymond turns to Amanda. "Unfortunately, we can't join you for dinner. We have other responsibilities. But rest assured we will return in the morning. Might even be able to help you plan your travels."

"That would be delightful. Thank you." Amanda gives them a grateful smile.

Raymond turns to the housekeeper. "Do you think you can give this poor woman a bed for the night? It would be a shame to feed her, only to turn her loose in the forest."

The housekeeper considers the request. "I'll have to ask Madam, of course. But she always is a gracious host. I'm sure we can come up with a spare bed."

Amanda bids the kind gentlemen goodbye then follows the housekeeper to the kitchen. There she finds a simmering iron kettle with a pot roast inside. There's also freshly baked bread. She eats ravenously. Between bites, she tells the maid about her travels.

But the maid, who never shares her name, responds minimally to each statement. Amanda realizes she has heard such tales before. Each arrival who washes in must spin a similar yarn.

When Amanda finishes her meal, she helps clear the dishes and washes her plate. Then she helps scrub the pots and pans.

This seems to impress the housekeeper. "You know," she says, "I think Madam might indeed enjoy meeting you this evening. I don't believe she's gone to bed yet. I'm going to leave you for a moment so I can inquire."

Amanda thanks her and stays in the kitchen. After a few minutes, her gaze drifts upward, along the glass walls and then to the huge windows embedded in the domed ceiling. At that moment, she realizes one of the most remarkable things about living in a glass house. At night, you can look up and see the stars.

# Chapter 4

## *The Pull of the Deep*

Victor Marius walks through the Boston neighborhood of Charlestown until he reaches the bank of the Mystic River. For a moment, he stands, staring into its dark waters. A half-filled wine jug dangles from his hand.

The jug was a hasty purchase the night before. A temporary lapse in judgment for the scientist – who thought he had given up this craving.

But the night was particularly lonely. Just hours before, he watched his one-time flame, Abigail, disappear into her new life. The doors to the convent swung closed behind her. He knows the two of them will never reconnect.

Victor looks down at the jug.

Their brief courtship seemed so right at the start, then so off-track as the days went on. But he would always remember it.

Yesterday had been a one-two punch. Since his scientific research wasn't paying the bills, he had taken a job as an electric lineman. But a few hours after Abigail departed, he learned his work hours on the electric poles were reduced. That was his reward for doing a job well. His team had been so fast and successful at stringing wires that he was told they needed to slow down. For the next few weeks, they could only offer his team a few hours of work.

So, the wine jug, when it caught his eye, seemed a bit too easy to pick up.

But after the first hour of drinking, he knew it held nothing for him.

He had gone deep beneath the cork before. Best not to take that ride again. Come morning, he promised he would rid himself of the demon before it moved in permanently.

So, here he is, beside the river.

He thinks once more of Abigail.

Then he thinks of Florence, his confidante before Abigail.

Ahh, Florence. Was she, perhaps, his biggest mistake of all?

Beautiful. Wealthy. Charming. Florence was smart and sweet. She was the total package, and most people would call him a fool for leaving her. But he did just that.

He looks at the jug again. He should not look too long, lest he decides to keep it.

With a long slinging underhand, he pitches the jug hard, then watches it arc over the water, landing with a splash. It bobs a bit, then drifts out of sight.

Temptation eliminated, he sets a new course and starts running. Running to get his body in order. Getting fit helped him find peace in the past. He'll count on that again.

His run eventually takes him to Boston's Back Bay, where he slows to a walk. He searches for the large brownstone that serves as the neighborhood police station. In the 900 block of Boylston Street, he spots it. The duty officer at the front desk notices him as he steps inside.

"Recruit?"

"I'm hoping so."

"They're expecting you."

Victor is directed to a room down the hall. There, he finds a Lieutenant seated behind a battered desk. The officer looks up.

"You Marius?" Checks a name on his blue sheet of paper. "Victor Marius?"

"That's me."

"All right. I understand you asked recently about signing up." The man's chair squeaks as he leans back. "What makes you want to be a police officer?"

Victor considers his response. "In truth? I need work. And you need good men, part-time."

The Lieutenant nods. "Just part time? You still have to do all the same reading and training. Turns out we have a couple of full-time slots available if you make the grade."

"I know. But part time works for me right now. What does the training involve?"

"Three days right here in this building. That's the classroom stuff. You need to read two manuals. There's a test after that. Then, let's see, a day at our shooting range in Dorchester. Then you need to learn the proper way to handle arrests. You know, what you say, how you act, the paperwork. A few other things. Toward the end, you spend a few days walking the streets with a couple of officers. After that, we assign you to someone new every week for about a month. That helps you get a range of experience."

Victor nods.

"That's it. A few weeks tops, assuming you have a brain. Good thing is you'll get your badge after just the first few days."

"And the pay?"

"Better than what you'll make sweeping streets. You ever been arrested?"

Victor shakes his head no.

"Ever been in the military?"

"Can't say as I have."

"That would certainly help get you hired. Ain't a requirement though. Ever been shot at? Been in any fights?"

"No. And yes."

"Did you win?"

"Most of the time."

The officer laughs and hands Victor some papers to fill out. He finishes quickly. "That's it?"

"We have your name. We'll do some checking. Police records and stuff. The class part is starting in a few days. We have three other guys so far. Just show up for the class and if we've been able to clear you by then, you can join 'em."

Victor nods. "Looking forward to it."

The officer looks him up and down. "So, tell me again? Why part time, and not full time?"

"I have some other things I'm working on. I do some work with electricity."

"That a fact? Fascinating. But it's dangerous damn stuff. So, what are you doing? Installing?"

"In a way. I run the wires down the streets. Right now, we're bringing them farther and farther from the generating plants. I just do the long haul. I don't wire houses or businesses or anything. But stringing wires isn't my main thing. I do research too. I have a small laboratory. Looking for new ways to use power. And some other things."

"Huh. Sounds interesting. But if you're here, my guess is it doesn't pay well."

Victor laughs. "No, I haven't found the magic formula yet to make myself rich."

The cop shrugs. "I don't really understand any of it. But, hey, good for you. Just make sure it doesn't cut into your training time or your duties. We'll see you in a few days."

# Chapter 5

## *The Keepers*


Jonathan Morgan has not seen Amanda in weeks. But he made a promise to her, and he takes that promise seriously. He keeps her puzzle box in a protected space, under the watchful eye of a friend.

Hat tipped forward to protect his face from the noonday sun, Jonathan knocks on the front door of that friend's brownstone.

Jasper Stokes answers the knock. He looks up and down the street before fully opening the door.

"Come in. Please."

Once Jonathan enters, Jasper looks around again, then closes and locks the door.

"Were you followed?"

"Of course not. I'm careful, and I haven't seen anyone suspicious in days."

Jasper ushers his friend into the parlor. "Still, we can't be too vigilant, given the number of times people have tried to steal this thing."

Jonathan waits as his friend retrieves a key. "Maybe we're being a bit silly. I mean, no one really knows what's inside the box. We could all be wasting our time, including any potential thieves."

Jasper unlocks a tall cabinet and retrieves a canvas mail sack. Reaching inside, he removes an object that's wrapped in strips of old bedsheet. After unraveling the cloth strips, he places Amanda's puzzle box in the middle of an oval tea table.

Jonathan examines the piece. "Wow. You've polished it. Very nice. The oil brings out all the woodgrains."

"Yes, quite. Makes for an interesting display piece, I think. Not that I could leave it in an open room right now."

"Spend any time playing with it? Any new discoveries?"

"No. I've tried, but I can only open it to the levels we've already reached. Frankly, I'm stymied."

Jonathan sits on the stuffed settee and pulls the puzzle box toward him. In a few minutes, he has it half-disassembled. Pieces are strewn about the table. "It would be wonderful if we could figure out the entire disassembly before Amanda comes to reclaim it. Imagine     the fun of showing her how all the levels open and showing her whatever we may find inside."

Jasper watches him work. "Yes, and knowing what's inside would be rewarding. Do you think she's actually coming back though?"

Jonathan raises an eyebrow. "Of course. Why wouldn't I think so?"

"Well, it's been weeks, right? No telegrams? No contact?"

"She's traveling. When we agreed to keep this box safe, she warned us she might be out of communication for quite some time. I'm glad we can provide safekeeping."

"I understand. Was just wondering." He watches Jonathan reach the point of disassembly they have already reached several times. His progress stops. He continues to struggle with the puzzle's next level. After a few moments, he sits back, then points to a frame-like decoration around the edge of that level. "So now, let's think about this. Why is that thin frame there, Jasper? It seems out of place. The other levels didn't have frames. I'll bet that slides. What do you think?"

"It's worth exploring."

Jonathan takes a flat letter opener and drags it along the edge of the frame. He manages to get the flat point of the opener behind the ridge of wood.

"That's it," Jasper whispers. "Slide it over. Righto, tiny gap there. Now see if you can get your thumbnail under it…"

There's a slight click. Their faces brighten, and the two men exchange a grin as the frame lifts away.

# Chapter 6

## *Devlin Alone*

At Western Union's main Boston office, the agent behind the counter can't help but stare at the red scar curling up Devlin Richard's cheek.

But Devlin is oblivious to the gaze. Instead, he's focused on a piece of paper he's just been handed. He unfolds the telegram, reads it, then sneers. The sneer only makes the scar seem more foreboding.

*Jeb Thomas. Contacting me? That bastard.* Devlin rubs his cheek. He thought Jeb had disappeared from his life. Gone for weeks. Now he's coming back? Apparently, he plans to just jump back into their dealings with no hesitation and no explanation of his absence.

Devlin's first thought is, well, *fuck him.*

Yet, with some trepidation, he realizes Jeb might still be useful. For Devlin, reconnecting could be a path out of his recent string of bad luck. Jeb's telegram hints the girl might be returning too. If Devlin wants to take another shot at nabbing the puzzle box, working through Jeb could be his best bet.

He thanks the gawking clerk and tucks the telegram into his pocket.

To clear his head, Devlin takes a walk. Hands in his pockets. Head down. Maybe this could be a welcome change of focus. Too often lately, his thoughts have revolved around Irene. That needs to change. Thinking of her just stokes his anger.

Irene who deserted him.

Irene who professed to love him, then stole his money and wrecked his plans.

Irene who simply disappeared.

At this point, he very much wants to destroy her out of pure revenge. But, strangely, he also wants to have her back. These mixed feelings seem foreign to a man who is used to treating every encounter as a transaction, while establishing few long-term relationships.

So why does he want her back in his life? Back in his bed? Back in all of his plans for tomorrow and beyond? The mixed feelings baffle him.

Fuck Irene, in oh so many ways.


He purposely strolls past Jonathan Morgan's home, where Amanda lived for those first weeks when she arrived in Boston. That's the place where Devlin was first able to steal the puzzle box, even though the police ended up confiscating it.

Not much to see here now. The old man isn't outside. Devlin scans the street. He knows Jonathan Morgan has friends nearby. He knows the old man has the box again because he picked it up from the police station. But there is no indication Morgan took it back to this house. That means a friend must be sheltering it. But Devlin can't break into and search every home in the neighborhood.

He absentmindedly strokes the red scar.

He hates to admit it, but Jeb is right. The key is to find and follow that woman, Amanda, when she returns. She'll eventually lead them both to the Puzzle Box.

He paces. Something is gnawing at him. There's one thing that doesn't fully add up. Why would Jeb bother to bring him back into his plan? Jeb could certainly follow the girl on his own. He could grab the box when he finds it and be gone without ever involving another person. So why would Jeb contact him?

Devlin mulls this over as he walks toward his home.

There can be only one reason. Based on the wording of his telegram, it's clear Jeb and the girl are now traveling separately. They were a close pair when they left. So, they must have had a falling out. That means, if they're both headed back to Boston, Jeb is chasing after her. Maybe he's hoping to patch things up. That could be why he needs someone else to do the theft. He doesn't want to come off as the bad guy.

Maybe, instead, maybe Jeb wants to be the hero?

*Interesting,* Devlin mutters to himself.

Up ahead, on the sidewalk, a child approaches. When he sees Devlin's face, he stops for a moment, then crosses the street. The

Southerner doesn't mind. He's become used to such reactions since his face got cut.

Instead, he plays some scenarios in his mind.

One: Jeb could do the reconnaissance work. Devlin will then snatch the box, from wherever it's being held, and the two of them will split the contents. That would be a workable scenario, but he doesn't trust Jeb.

Two: Jeb might set him up to take a fall. After the box is stolen, he could make sure Devlin is caught. The box would be returned to the girl, and Jeb might come off looking like a hero to her. And if he and the girl end up getting back together, Jeb would end up with access to the box and Devlin will be out of the picture.

Devlin reaches home and sits in the only chair in his room. Feet on his bed, he stares at the wall.

He supposes there could be a third possibility. If Jeb manages to reconnect with the girl and patch things up before the box is ever stolen, then he won't need Devlin's services at all. But so far that doesn't seem to be the case.

He weighs the possibilities over and over in his mind. The more he thinks about it, the angrier he becomes. He's convinced Jeb contacted him with one purpose only – to make him a patsy as he tries to win back his woman.

*No. This won't do. This won't do at all.*

Devlin will have to proceed very carefully from here. His main goal now is to locate the box and to keep it all for himself. He'll use Jeb as a tool if needed. But he'll start by seeing what the shopkeeper, Chen Lu, knows.

In the meantime, Devlin plans to head over to Beacon Hill after the sun sets. He's noticed two homes there that have been dark for the past few nights. Maybe he can slip inside. Maybe he can find a few more valuable items to stash in his carpetbag.

# Chapter 7

## *A Friend in Need*

Professor Alton approaches Victor's brick building and knocks twice on the front door. There is no answer, so he gives the big door a push and walks in.

At first, the place seems empty. Then he finds Victor upstairs in his loft, fully dressed, lying on his bed, staring at the boards in the ceiling.

The professor peers over the top of the loft's built-in ladder. "What's going on? No work today?"

"Work has been cut back quite a bit. Let's just say I'm weighing other options."

"I see," the professor nods. "I understand you are seeking work as a police officer? That's a change for you. And from what I've heard, Victor, you haven't been feeling well for a few days. Including doing a little drinking. Can I take you to see a doctor?"

Victor shakes his head. "I don't quite know what's ailing me, but I don't think any doctor has a cure."

Alton brushes some dust off the floor of the loft. It looks like it hasn't been cleaned in some time. "And what do you think it might be, this thing that's ailing you?"

"Melancholy? Who knows!" Victor points his finger at the sloped ceiling. "You see these boards, Doc? All those weeks ago, after I nearly drowned at sea, I awoke on a French ship. I think I told you about that. Well, one of the first things I remember is staring at some boards of the ship – just a few inches in front of my face. Sort of like this. I remember trying to figure out where I was, what those boards were, and what the hell was going on."

Victor takes a deep breath and continues. "Well, guess what? Here I am, back on land. I'm whole and healthy again, and now we're at the other end of the summer. And guess what? I'm still laying beneath a row of boards, trying to figure out what the hell is going on." He sighs and shakes his head. "I've tried to do many things since coming back to Boston. But I get no traction. Now I'm taking a job as a cop, not because I have a strong calling for police work, but simply because they were hiring. All my other work, all *our* work exploring radio? That's come to naught. I've made zero money from it. So, if I'm taking work I don't even care about, where does that leave me? I might as well still be floating on the sea."

The professor looks troubled. "I don't know what to say, my boy." He climbs back downstairs, rummages through the icebox, and fixes the pair some lunch.

He coaxes Victor down to the main floor and they eat a simple meal of apples, cheese, and some stale hardtack. Victor looks longingly at the spot where his wine jug used to sit.

Professor Alton tries a different approach.

"You may not want to continue with your radio research, son, but I certainly need to keep going with my own research and tests. And to do that, I could use your help."

"My help? What for?"

"Damn it, Victor, we were going to test the radio transmissions together, you and I. You know we need two antennas and two sets of equipment. We need to be separated by a great distance. I need your skills."

"Sorry. My tower is gone now, damaged by fire and wind. I can't offer you help for anything, professor."

"Oh, but you can," Alton chides. "I still have my system, and we will just build another for you to use. And maybe a smaller portable antenna too."

Victor shrugs.

"And I could use some design help. I know the basics of your new ideas. They are better than you think. We can build an improved system in a matter of days. So, this weekend. That's when I'm setting up my tower. I do hope you'll be there."

With that, Professor Alton takes a final piece of cheese from the plate, pats Victor on the shoulder, and exits the building.

Before closing the door, the old man pops his head back inside. "By the way, Victor, the Institute has been talking about funding a new assistant professorship. They are looking for someone who will focus on electrical engineering. Now, I'm not sure if the new opening will come to pass or be fully funded, but if it does, I'd like to recommend you for the position."

Victor considers this for a moment. "Would I have access to what I need – to continue my research?"

"More than you've dreamed."

He doesn't change his expression. But he does nod.

Victor spends the rest of the day doing... not much of anything. But that evening, he finally settles down at his table, where he makes some measurements and a few hasty sketches. If Professor Alton really does intend to continue his radio research, Victor feels obligated to update his design. Halfway through a drawing, he smiles, knowing full well this is exactly what the old man intended.

At about midnight, Victor hits a dead end. While he's very satisfied with his new plans, there's an issue with the transmitter that troubles him. Something about the way the signal dissipates. It's too rapid. In theory, it won't let him achieve the long-distance signal reach he desires.

He paces, reviewing the designs and potential results in his mind. After an hour of considering the idea from different viewpoints, he comes up with a solution, but he realizes he wants Tesla's input on the concept. Victor decides not to wait for the U.S. mail. He wants to take his drawings directly to New York, just for a day trip. He wants to review the schematic with Tesla – face to face.

# Chapter 8

## *The Fallen*

In a few minutes, Mrs. Lethe's housekeeper returns. "Yes," she says. "Madam would be pleased to meet you. Do step this way. But please keep in mind she has not had a good day. Not at all."

Amanda follows the woman down a remarkable corridor. Candles hang from sconces set between window frames. Light reflects across the array of glass panes, making it seem like she's passing through a tunnel of fireflies.

When they enter Mrs. Lethe's study, they find her standing at the far end of the room, staring out the window. The housekeeper steps forward.

"Miss Amanda Grant, ma'am. Here to meet you."

The old woman says nothing. The housekeeper steps back and exits the room, leaving them alone.

They stand in silence for nearly a minute. At last, Mrs. Lethe speaks. She does not turn to look at Amanda.

"You'll have to forgive me, my dear. This has been a dreadful day. We had an intruder who caused some commotion. He was caught stealing from one of the men who reside in this compound. I understand you met him."

"Yes, ma'am," Amanda responds. "I met two men. They were kind to me. They brought me here."

"I'm glad they helped you. Unfortunately, the theft of his suit didn't turn out to be the worst of it. This intruder is still here and I'm unsure of how to deal with him." Mrs. Lethe sighs. "But no matter. Here we are now. Let's make the most of it."

She finally turns and extends a hand to Amanda. "Charmed to meet you, my dear. Please, do tell me how you came to be wandering through our isolated domain."

She invites Amanda to sit with her. They settle into upholstered armchairs. Burgundy velvet. Gold trim. Between them, a low bronze table holds a silver tea set. Mrs. Lethe pours. The tea slides like thin honey into the cups.

Amanda begins her tale, backing up a bit to include events from the time she reached Montana until she crossed the Mississippi and came up the muddy bank, battered and lost, not far from here. The old woman listens, mesmerized.

"So, you don't have a way home now? No horse? No money? Nothing?"

"No, ma'am. I do not. I'm hoping maybe to find work. Just enough work to purchase a few things, including a ticket home."

"Home … to Boston?"

"Yes. To Boston. How did you know?"

The grand lady smiles. "You do have a trace of an accent."

Amanda asks more questions. She wonders how the house came to be built. Mrs. Lethe tells her own story, detailing how her husband came to this land from far away, intent on seeking his fortune and building this domain. "In his homeland, they call him Sir now. But he was not awarded that title until much later in his life." She laughs. "His homeland had no use for him at all when he was young. It was only after he came here to prove his worth that they even noticed him. He used his success to fund charities back home. That's when they finally recognized him for the good man he was."

"Was? Does that mean he's… no longer around?"

"Oh, he endures. But you won't see him. He travels. I do miss him when he is gone."

Amanda gives her a sympathetic look.

"You may have noticed, Abraham has a fascination with the new architecture. This kind of building style has flourished in England under Victoria. Well, I suppose it has flourished in this country too. The glass. The arches. All the ornamentation. A bit gaudy for my tastes, but he loves it all."

"Yes, ma'am. It really is quite remarkable."

"He had a particular interest in elaborate greenhouses. They were the rage for a few years. London's Crystal Palace and the like. All manner of decorative iron and glass. I suppose it gave folks a way to bring a bit of summer indoors during bleak winters. If you look around here, you will see some remnants of that. Some flowers can still be found along the edges, a few palm trees in the corners, and an indoor fountain."

"Or models of planets," Amanda smiles.

The old woman laughs. "Yes. Or planets. My husband was quite the eccentric. And quite the grand architect. This whole place grew from his first garden. Abraham and I loved it out here in the country. Now, these tall windows let us see it all. There are no real roads to here. So, we would travel by creek. Then we'd hike. He paid the local boys great piles of money to haul the building materials out here. Some on horses. Some just on their backs. It took years."

Mrs. Lethe smiles, lost, for a bit, in happy memories. "We first stayed here in the warmer months. Then we spent more and more time here as we grew older. He would hunt and fish. Besides the house, we built a barn. Then some outbuildings. We still raise sheep and pigs. Silly things, pigs are."

"It all sounds wonderful."

"Yes. For us it was. Still is. This is where I live full time now. Our other homes mostly stand empty. This is my world. The only visitors we receive are those who end up here by accident, such as yourself. Sometimes from floods. Sometimes because they wander in through the wilderness. If you were trying to find this place on purpose, I'm not sure that you could." She takes a long sip of tea. "It is a splendid isolation."

Amanda asks more questions – about the giant bookshelves and some of the artwork. Mrs. Lethe has stories about many things in the room. She's proud of her domain. Grateful to have someone with whom she can talk.

"I do have to ask," Amanda adds with a hint of nervousness, "who are all the other people I've seen here? There must be dozens of them."

"Likely more. Temporary visitors dear, much like yourself."

"Lost?"

"Many of them are. Yes."

Amanda is perplexed. "Some of those people look like they've been here for quite a while. Do some people choose to stay? I know it may be challenging to leave, but I've already been told some people do find their way out if they choose to."

Mrs. Lethe looks her in the eyes. "Well, that's the great notion, isn't it? *Effort*. Circumstances may set one adrift and push one aside. Yet some people still find their way while others repeatedly try and fail. There are folks who spend their lives being washed into the gutter time and again. For them, efforts can be futile. Cruel. Overwhelming." She leans closer. "To some, I suppose it may no longer seem worth any exertion."

Amanda blinks. "I understand. But I have to know. Do most people eventually leave here?"

"I think they all hope to. Yes."

Amanda considers this for a moment. "Well, I certainly hope to."

Mrs. Lethe nods. "Then I hope you will find your way. But I do understand that for some people it's easier to live like a seed, dear. To simply float where the wind carries you. Or the water. Some people simply settle wherever it is they drift. Gutter flowers. Right? They bloom where they are planted."

Amanda's eyes widen. "My grandfather used to say that."

The old woman smiles. "Did he?"

They look at each other for a moment. "And did you?" Mrs. Lethe continues. "Did you bloom where you were planted?"

Amanda shakes her head. "I think my grandfather, if he was still around, would say I did not. I think he would say I wandered off. I went to look for something better, but I never found it."

"Yes. Pity." The old woman smiles. Amanda feels troubled even as she believes the old woman's smile to be sincere.

Mrs. Lethe studies her. "But you should know, dear, I see no turpitude in electing to move on before you bloom. Many souls do climb up and out of their gutter. So why not try? If you have no real roots – the wind, the weather, other fates; they all can move a person toward a new destiny. Take my dear Abraham. He certainly didn't stay where he was planted, and he found great things." She pats Amanda's hand. "But here, in this great river valley, we have seen many who were washed away like dust from the road. And here they collect. Like a puddle in the rain."

Amanda remains silent. She looks up again through the glass windows. Toward the stars. But now she sees mostly clouds.

"Sometimes," Amanda says with a shaking voice, "even for people who break free, luck and fate push too hard. I'm sure you've seen that. At some point, when circumstances beat a person down, just choosing to stay down... it seems... less taxing. Maybe less risky." Amanda feels tears forming in her eyes. She fights them.

"I understand, dear."

"I don't think I want to be here. When I left home, I never expected to find so many dead ends. And I certainly never dreamed of finding myself in a massive one like this." She holds her head in her hands. "I feel tired. I don't know what's happening."

Mrs. Lethe places a hand on Amanda's shoulder. "Nothing is really a dead end if you are... willing to overcome whatever knocks you down and pushes you into the unknown."

Amanda stares ahead. "How many times?"

"Oh, my dear. I fully understand how getting up each time becomes an overwhelming burden."

Amanda feels her head droop. She is spent and dizzy and fights the urge to close her eyes.

"I make a promise to the people who end up here," Mrs. Lethe confides. "They always are welcome to stay. I'm well off. That is my gift to them. The property is sprawling and most guests don't trouble me at all, no matter how they arrive."

"That's very kind of you."

"Nonsense. It's my duty to nurture those who find purchase here. You saw many lost souls on your way in. I'm quite sure you are able to tell which ones might be just passing through versus those who may never leave."

"Yes, I think I can."

"But I do ask, for anyone who stays, that they deal with any encumbrances that may have followed them here. Obsessions. Lusts. Addictions. All of those can be the very things that continue to pull a person down, no? They must be named. Faced. Subjugated."

"I see."

"You know," Mrs. Lethe adds, "that is the saddest of all. When someone's personal demons have so consumed them that they don't realize how their lives have changed. Drinking. Dreaming. Drifting."

She leans in, whispering to Amanda. "And sometimes, I've noticed, people are simply poisoned by hate. Hate for circumstance. Disdain for past lovers. Parents. Old friends. Hate for anyone or anything different. That's the most heartbreaking. I see them wandering in circles in my fields. Arms waving. Ground down by life and shouting into the wind."

She looks intently at Amanda. "Or hate for a man or a woman, even as they feel drawn to them."

Amanda looks away. "I don't think most people start out hating. Especially not hating men or women in general. But in life, things... happen."

"Yes. That's true. Things do happen."

Amanda rises and paces. There is nothing to see outside the tall windows. Just blackness. Not even her own reflection looks back. "Sometimes, people just need to find a safer place. At least for a while."

"Yes, my dear. Sometimes they do. And is that what you want? To stay here? To stay safe?"

"I don't know."

Mrs. Lethe looks into the distance. She's steadfast. Inscrutable. "You have a complicated journey ahead of you. You've been pushed past the point where most people give up. So, I very much commend you for making it this far."

Amanda takes a deep breath. "I have never given up."

Then her dizziness returns. She fights the feeling that she is toppling backward, never quite reaching the floor. It feels like floating on the river. Or laying wet and hopeless in the dirt where she first fell.

"And the anger?"

"I'm not angry," Amanda replies. "Just disappointed."

"In what, dear?"

"In myself."

"I see. Why is that?"

"Because I relied on people when I shouldn't have. Because I trusted and I shouldn't have. Because..." she holds her hands up to her mouth.

"And you think that's your fault?"

Amanda looks away. "How do I make it stop?"

"Anger? You can simply dwell on it – but just long enough to see the folly of it. Then you can let it die."

Amanda's vision blurs. "I think I should rest."

Mrs. Lethe rings a bell, and the housekeeper returns. The next thing Amanda knows, she is stretched out atop a thick green-and-brown comforter. There are flowers at its edges. The window is ajar, and the dew seems to have made its way inside. Night birds sing softly in the swamps, and the flowers on the comforter undulate in the wind.

# Chapter 9

## *Off the Scent*

Jeb's coach drops him in front of a tiny train station. The rail line turns out to be a private spur connecting just four villages. The last stop is a slightly larger station shared with the Ohio and Mississippi Railroad. Jeb only waits a couple of hours to board a train for Cincinnati.

As they travel, Jeb notices the train occasionally chugs along the rim of the old Cincinnati and Whitewater Canal. The remnants of that waterway remain visible. A towpath. A small lock with gates now hanging askew. He sees spillways from streams that once helped fill the ditch. Not long ago, this canal was still functional and active. He marvels at how quickly railroads displaced other methods of travel.

So be it, he thinks. From a labor standpoint, the canals often exploited their workers. Railroads do too, but there are unions there. Folks like Jeb are working to make sure exploitation is a thing of the past.

As the train pulls into Cincinnati, Jeb jumps from the doorway before the cars come to a stop. He heads directly to the terminal's telegraph office and sends Devlin another message. It's frustrating that he can't receive any messages in return. He can't even be sure his telegrams are being read. He can only hope.

The message he sends is to reconfirm his return to Boston and to say he's not been able to pick up new clues about where Amanda might be headed. He again asks Devlin to watch for her. He also asks Devlin to send a reply to the next major station on his route.

After paying for the telegram, Jeb grabs supper from a vendor selling strips of fried bison and salt potatoes. Then he heads back inside, to the ticket window.

"One way to Buffalo please." The woman behind the counter takes his money and slides the fat yellow ticket through a gap in the glass.

# Chapter 10

## *What Lies Within*

"This time," Devlin mutters to himself, "Chen is going to talk to me. He damn well better, if he knows what's good for him."

Just 10 minutes prior, Devlin learned shopkeeper Chen Lu was released from jail after posting a rather substantial bond. Chen had been arrested, weeks prior, and he sat in his cell ever since. But now, suddenly, he's free.

How?

Devlin wants answers. First, where did Chen get the money? Second, did his sudden good fortune have anything to do with the missing puzzle box?

In the brief time Devlin and Chen worked together, the box was briefly in their possession and they both tried to get it open – not just to satisfy their curiosity, but to possibly find something of value inside. Maybe diamonds. Maybe gold.

It may not matter where the box is now. If Chen managed to get it open before he was arrested, before the police confiscated the box, then he may have kept whatever he found inside. He may have hidden it before the box was ever impounded by the police. If that's true, finding the box again might mean nothing.

Maybe Chen was only waiting in jail for some associate to get to the hidden stash and to convert it into dollars to help make bail.

If Devlin's suspicions turned out to be true, it meant Chen Lu had been quite dishonest with him. And that would not do at all.

With a determined walk, Devlin navigates the streets toward Chen's shop. He crosses near Canal and Haverhill streets, where he's learned to go slow and approach cautiously. Train tracks converge here from different angles. Pedestrians must look multiple ways, to make sure no trains are bearing down.

As Devlin looks across the street, he spies a woman wearing a dress with a familiar pattern. It stops him dead. His gaze follows the woman until she turns a corner. He glimpses her profile and feels an angry chill.

That's her. That's Irene.

He wasn't sure if she's still in Boston, but there she is, the one who took his money and disappeared. The one who broke his heart.

His fist clenches into a ball. His eyes narrow. He starts to take a step in her direction, only to hear the loud screech of a train whistle. Instinctively he jumps back, and the iron front corner of a locomotive misses him by mere inches. Devlin paces back and forth, trying to keep his eye on Irene. But that's difficult through the gaps of the rushing freight train. By the time the last car passes, she's out of sight.

Running to the corner, Devlin looks up and down. There's a rat's nest of roads near this intersection and she could have walked in any direction, or into any of the shops. Discouraged but still hopeful, he follows the sidewalks for several minutes. He looks into windows and up alleys. But the trail has gone cold. He makes a mental note to return here soon, to look for her again. But for now, he must focus on Chen Lu's shop.


When Devlin arrives at the shop, he finds it empty. The front windows are coated in white soap. Old newspapers cover the glass of the front door. Devlin isn't surprised. When the law discovered Chen Lu was selling stolen goods, they cleaned him out.

Devlin walks to the rear alley and finds the back door propped open for ventilation. The old man is in his back rooms. With nowhere else to go, he must be living there.

Devlin draws his knife and steps inside.

"You," Chen Lu exclaims as he turns.

"Yeah. Me. And you know what I'm here for."

Chen Lu shakes his head. "I don't have. Still at police, I think."

Devlin kicks the door closed behind him. He drives his knife down into the counter. It makes a threatening thud followed by a short vibration.

"I know you don't have the box anymore. I only care if you were able to open it."

"I know nothing."

It takes a while, and some rough treatment. But Devlin manages to extract a bit of information. He's not sure if he believes the old man's story, but Chen claims he was close to opening the final level, and he was convinced something of value was stored inside. But he hastily reassembled it when he heard customers entering his shop. And he put it in the safe that he was never able to reopen. When police raided his shop, they took several things, including his safe and the box inside.

"What about the bail money, Chen? Where did you get that?" He sees the old man's eyes gaze upwards to a shelf. On that shelf, barely visible near the ceiling, sit several opium pipes and some boxes.

"The police did not find everything. I have associates. We had things to sell."

Devlin pushes the old man into a chair, yanks his knife from the table, and points it at him.

"Why did you try to tell me the police still have the box? We both know they don't. We both know it was given back."

"To who?"

"That's what I'm doing! Trying to find it!" He kicks out the legs of the chair and lets Chen fall to the ground.

Devlin continues his questioning, but the effort brings nothing new. Eventually he storms out of the shop, realizing Jeb was right when he sent his telegrams. The only way to get the box now is through Amanda, if she ever shows up.

So, where the hell is she?

# Chapter 11

## *The Arrangement*

Amanda sits in the kitchen of the big house, enjoying a wonderful breakfast. Eggs, ham, and a fresh chunk of bread that she tore from a round loaf.

Mrs. Lethe enters wearing a green-and-orange Japanese robe, cinched tight around her waist. Curtain-like sleeves trail behind her.

"I trust you slept well, my dear?"

"I did, indeed," Amanda responds. "I thought I might never wake up."

Mrs. Lethe pours herself some tea. Hand-thrown clay cup. Painting of a bright sun on its face. She joins Amanda, and they make idle chit-chat. The weather. The kitchen. The animals in the surrounding woods.

Then Amanda asks the old woman a direct question. "You had a forlorn look when I first came into your room. You said it was a bad day for you. Why was that, ma'am?"

The woman gives a slight laugh. "Well, as you know, yesterday we apprehended a trespasser on the grounds. It's made me a bit concerned, and we are still trying to decide what to do with him."

"I'm sorry to hear that, ma'am. Do you consider him a threat?"

"What makes you ask, dear?"

"Well… Because strangers do arrive here on occasion, right? Not often, but they do drift in, just like me."

She knows she has Mrs. Lethe's attention, but the old woman's expression remains inscrutable.

"So," Amanda continues, "since you seem quite welcoming to most of us, why do you think of this particular visitor a trespasser?"

"Because…" Mrs. Lethe takes a deep breath. "Because his arrival is not accidental. Because he is not here just for himself. He's following someone."

She raises an eyebrow as she looks at Amanda, and the young woman sighs. "Oh no. Unbelievable."

"So, you may know him?"

"Unfortunately, I think I may."

"Indeed. I suspected he might have come here for you, this trespasser. You and he showed within hours of each other."

Amanda closes her eyes. In her mind, she pictures Jeb. He must have managed to cross the river too. "I'm so sorry. Yes, he must have followed me. I don't know how. But he managed to do so. And I do think I know who it is."

Mrs. Lethe shakes her head. "No, dear. While he may have followed you, I do not think that you know him. At least, you haven't met him face to face. I can assure you of that."

"How would you know that?"

"Because I think I know who this individual is. Or what he is. I can say this is not like anything you have ever seen." She leans forward, voice dropping to a whisper. "Not like anything I've seen in a long time. And I promise you, it's indeed cause for concern."

Amanda shifts uneasily in her chair. "All right. Can you explain what you mean by that?" She had thought the trespasser must be Jeb. But when Mrs. Lethe describes the cunning strangeness and threatening manner of the visitor, Amanda quickly changes her mind. Instead, she decides the visitor must be the forlorn and unstable Ephraim, who threatened her and then followed her from the riverboat. If that is the case, she's glad the threat has been contained in the barn.

"You don't believe me. I can tell," Mrs. Lethe says. "You still think you know who it is out there in the barn. But I will predict you have never met this one face to face. Maybe by your own choice. That said, you likely have felt his impact for years. He is cunning. He's deceptive. And prone to triggering deep emotions. So, that is why I'm trying to warn you and prepare you. Until now, you have only felt his influence. But now here he is. In the flesh."

"I don't understand."

"You need to go to him. See him for what he is. Deal with him, even if it ends you."

Amanda blinks. She did not expect this. She found a welcome bit of respite in this strange place, and now she is being given a task with no real instructions, and a potentially dangerous outcome. She looks back at Mrs. Lethe.

"Well, you said he's naked. So, it shouldn't be hard to see him for what he is."

The old woman laughs. "What you will see will shock you. And not because of that." She frowns. Drops her voice low again. "You cannot take this meeting lightly, dear. I dare say it's a meeting you have very much avoided until now. And because of that, the threat has grown."

"Well, if it is who I think it is, I have only known him for a short period of time. And while I might want to avoid meeting him, I certainly don't fear a meeting. We already have parted ways."

Mrs. Lethe tilts her head a bit. "You still seem convinced it's someone you know? Go on."

"There was a second man who also followed me. His name is Ephraim, and I met him on a work boat. When we first met, I was hiding. I was dressed like a man. So, he thought I was someone else. He grew angry and started following me when he discovered I am a woman. But I don't fear him. I know of his broken mind and his eccentric personality. It's unfortunate. But he is manageable."

"You sincerely believe it's one of those two men, don't you?"

Amanda nods. "I mean, who else might it be?"

The old woman stares at her. "We all have *things* that follow us. From the choices we have made – some more dangerous than others. Often, we fail to recognize that." She places the tips of her fingers together. Carefully choosing her next words. "If we are lucky, these things, these entities, stay at the margins of our lives. We never need to confront."

"I don't quite fathom, ma'am. I… "

"Why are you here, Amanda? How did you end up here?"

"I've told you my story."

"Indeed, you have. But you have not fully answered that question. You have not answered to yourself."

"Ma'am?"

Mrs. Lethe shakes her head. "No matter. Let's just talk about what's out in the barn. Why do you think that suit of clothes was stolen in the first place? The one out in the barn? He was following you, dear, but he managed to arrive here ahead of you and he wanted to quickly blend in. But those two men caught him stealing. That greatly complicated his efforts.

"They chased the intruder, intending to take back what was stolen. It was just circumstance that they managed to corner him near the pig pens, and quite unfortunate for all that he slipped and fell a few times before hopping the fence and running into the barn. Silly place for him to go. No easy escape. Mr. Crowley and his friend Mr. Purling grabbed him and tied him to one of the horse-stall gates. Then they came in here, asking me what they should do."

"My guess is that you told them to just take back the suit," Amanda says. "I think that's when I first met the pair. They were leaving the barn and carrying the filthy clothes."

"Yes, and the suit is likely ruined," Mrs. Lethe laments. "Soaked through with foul waste."

The conversation lapses into silence as Mrs. Lethe looks impatient.

"So, he's still out there in the barn?" Amanda asks.

"They left him tied out there. As I said, he must still be dealt with."

Amanda smooths out the wrinkles on her dress. "Why are you telling me this?"

"Since he was following you, dear, this might be an opportune time for you to deal with him, given his situation. Go. Find out what he wants."

"I don't care what he wants. I want nothing to do with him."

"Then you must be the one who tells him that."

Mrs. Lethe rings a bell and asks for a pair of buckets, some soap powder, and a lamp. She hands them all to Amanda. "I believe this quarrelsome confrère in the barn is named Gaap. I can't say how I know this, but believe me, he is not someone to be trifled with. So please, Amanda, go and confront your visitor. See if you can clean the mess that he has made. For both of you. If we are not able to evict him, then at least he won't remain in his current state."

Amanda takes the buckets and walks through the house, then onto the wide back porch. She stands for a minute, just staring at the barn. It seems much farther across the field than she remembers. It had been a bright and cheerful morning, but now it's impossibly dark, almost like late evening. There are no lights showing from any of the outbuildings. There is no illumination on the path to the barn.

Taking a deep breath, she lifts a lamp from a nearby table and lights it. Then, she takes her first cautious step on a trek across the yard.

# Chapter 12

## *A Father's Plea*

Victor didn't invite Howard Gatwick to visit his home. Yet, there he is, walking through Victor's lab. Stepping with purpose. Examining pieces of equipment and looking like a rich man completely out of his element.

"Yes. Yes, indeed, Victor. This is an interesting place you have here. Florence would be, hmm, intrigued. Yes, that's the word."

Victor masks his skepticism. "Would she?"

Since the day he broke things off with the charming and beautiful Florence, Victor has not laid eyes on her, nor her father. He assumed the old man would be happy to see him out of the picture. Many men had designs on Howard's daughter, and he clearly sought to guide her toward the more wealthy and well-connected suitors. Yet, here he is, dropping by Victor's lab unannounced.

"So, what brings you here, sir?"

Howard looks up toward the roof. He squints at the narrow sleeping loft. "Hmm… Right. Well, let me cut to the chase, lad. Florence has not been the same since you stopped being… well, her beau. She's been distant. Very quiet. I've never seen anything like it. It is a troublesome mood. I came here today to talk with you because, frankly, I want my bubbly and engaged daughter back. Does that make sense?"

Victor takes a deep breath. "It does. Florence deserves to be happy, and I'm sorry to hear that she's not."

"Hmm. Yes."

Victor slides a pair of chairs out from his meager table. Offers coffee from his stove. It smells strong. Burnt. Howard sips it and doesn't seem to notice.

"I'm a bit confused though, sir. What, exactly, are you asking of me?"

Howard sets his cup on the table. "I'm not sure yet. I suppose I just wanted you to know how she's been feeling, Victor. Florence is quite a catch. An amazing catch, actually. And here she is, apparently still smitten with you."

Victor nods. "I was smitten with her too, sir. It's too bad things didn't work out."

The wealthy investor takes a deep breath, followed by a long exhale. "Yes, well, about that. I'm sure we can come to terms."

"Terms?"

The old man leans forward. "Last time we talked, Victor, I was a bit harsh. Definitely wanted to bring you on board, didn't I? Into one of my businesses. I think you would have been great there. I still do."

Victor remains silent.

"But you wanted to stay right here, doing..." He looks around the big workspace. "Well, doing whatever it is you do here."

Victor gives a skeptical look, then focuses on his workbench.

Howard backtracks. "Look, that didn't come out right. I understand you are involved with an important new industry. I can see you are firmly entrenched with your experiments. That's grand."

He leans closer. Gestures with his hands. "I guess what I'm trying to say is I understand not all men want to delve deeply into the business side of things. Nor should they. So, while I don't understand this new technology, I'm willing to talk with you more about it. If I learn more about it, I may even be interested in investing in it." He takes a deep breath. "May I be frank?"

"Please do."

"This building is an old space, son. Your tools are old. The windows are cracked and taped. It's going to be cold as hell in here come winter. I can see you're struggling."

"That part is quite true, unfortunately."

"Yet, from our limited conversations, I know you have revolutionary ideas. I know you have the attention of professors and more. I can see the direction the world is heading. It's clear that everyone wants electricity now, and the whole world is starting to intersect with the very things you're working on." He leans in and confides in a low voice. "I even did a little reading on this 'radio' technology you mentioned. Fascinating stuff. Can it be made to work? Who knows? But if so, I think it could change everything."

"I like to think it will. And I can tell you, sir, radio is already a reality. At least for short distances. I know it can be made to reach much farther. That's my current challenge."

The old man nods. "Well, with the right patent, long-range radio could be quite a valuable thing."

"A patent? It's a spark that creates a wave. It's physics. So, that's not really patentable."

"Ahh, but it may be. You see, Victor, whatever equipment you build to create that spark. That can be patented. Leveraged. Branded. And then sold en masse. And when you improve it, you patent the next versions too. You must think big for things like this, Victor. And your stake has to go into the ground quite early in the game."

Victor raises an eyebrow. "And what if those things never pay off? Do I abandon them? Just focusing on the money alone ends up pulling me away from what I'm trying to learn."

Howard sighs. "Yes, yes. I understand that. And I'd be lying if I said I didn't have an issue with that approach. But I believe you can do both, with the right backing. I respect you, Victor, and that means none of this is insurmountable. I want you to be successful, and I want Florence to be happy. She's all I have. And I know she seemed at her very happiest when she was with you."

Victor looks toward the ceiling for several moments. Then he starts laughing. "You know, for the price of just two of her dresses, you could probably fund my work for six months."

Howard picks up his coffee cup. Offers a little salute. "Oh, you are quite right on that account, lad. That girl has terribly expensive tastes." After a long sip, he adds, "By the way, I heard through a councilman friend that your name is on the list of new police recruits. I must say that surprised me. I think you could be a fine officer, but I know you want to be right here. I suspect you're only taking that job for the money."

Victor doesn't answer.

"So, my good man, it seems you are not totally against doing something other than research to earn your keep. Hm?"

Victor looks Howard in the eyes. "I guess being a part-time cop feels like a different way to be of service. To the whole community. I doubt being a businessman behind a desk would ever give me that same feeling."

Howard gives a skeptical smirk. "The world is run by men sitting behind desks, son. You'd be surprised at the amount of good you can do there. If you do well, then you can choose to give money to charities. Do that a few times and a feeling of wholesomeness floods right in."

They talk for another 20 minutes. Victor explains that he and Florence are unlikely to mend the rift that formed between them. But he's not opposed to seeing her again.

"Dinner then? Next week? Our place?"

"No, sir."

"No?"

"I'd prefer Florence contact me herself. Maybe that's silly. But I'm not chasing her. One of the last things she said to me is 'men don't break up with me, Victor.' But I did make that break. So, it may seem silly, but going back to her would just prove she was right all along, no?"

Howard chuckles. "Ah, you young people. Making life so complicated. But..." He stands, picks up his hat, and shakes Victor's hand. "I guess that's fair enough. I will tell her exactly what you said. Next move is up to her."

Victor sees Howard to the door. Then, when he's alone, he raises his eyebrows and shakes his head.

# Chapter 13

## *The Easy Ones*

If there's one thing Devlin Richards has learned since slipping into Boston, it's that several small crimes are less risky than focusing on bigger but more unpredictable jobs.

*Stealing small.* That's what he calls it. It takes more time. And if he comes up empty, it can be frustrating. But small and stealthy reduces the risk of getting his face sliced open again, or having to dodge bullets.

Stealing small is now how he occupies his evenings. Tools left outside by a forgetful craftsman? Devlin helps himself. Horses that can be stolen on one side of the city and sold on the other? Quick money. He's learned which pawnshops buy things with no questions asked.

Stealing small is a living. It's not a great one, but it's helping Devlin regain his financial footing. He's even learned to stealthily help himself to fruit and vegetables from the farmer's market.

It's already dark as Devlin returns from one such outing. He has apples crammed into his pockets and a new leather coat slung over his shoulder.

As he walks, he thinks about Irene.

Devlin continues to feel like he sees her occasionally. Always at a distance. A ghost he can never catch. A familiar dress or shoe? His heart races for a moment. But it's never her. And now he can't stop looking.

As he walks along a dark city street, a slight noise catches his ear. He stops and listens. It's a whimpering sound. It seems to be coming from the base of a nearby fence. Is it a person? An animal? Frowning, he walks to the fence, then walks its length. It's a seven-foot-tall barrier. About twenty-five feet long. Solid board. No gaps.

The sound is definitely coming from an animal. A tiny one.

Devlin backtracks and finds the source. There's a space, in one spot, where the ground drops away. The boards there don't quite reach the dirt. He peers into the opening, but it's black.

49

Devlin reaches for the top of the fence and pulls himself up. Looking over the top, he sees something that makes him chuckle. There's a mother dog lying in a pile of leaves – her back to the fence. She's just a mangy street mutt, dirty white and mottled brown. She is lying on her side, nursing four pups whose eyes have yet to open. Devlin sees tiny flaps for ears and pink noses the size of pencil erasers.

He can still hear the whining, but it's not coming from the pups he sees. He leans in more so he can see the other side of the hole at the bottom of the fence. There must be a fifth pup – one that rolled into the hole.

*Stupid dog*, Devlin mutters to himself.

He drops back down. On the sidewalk, he crouches on hands and knees. He clears away rocks and grass from the small opening and inserts his arm. He eventually finds a tiny paw, grasps it, and pulls.

There's a slight yelp. Devlin manages to wiggle and tug the tiny puppy out of its dirt prison. Once free, it nuzzles his hand, looking for milk.

Devlin walks to the middle of the street. He brushes away dirt and examines the dog under the moonlight. It looks unhurt. Boy pup. Quite lucky to be rescued.

He temporarily removes his stolen apples, puts the puppy in his pocket and pulls himself back up to the fence top, higher this time, bracing one forearm on the edge. He pulls the pup from his pocket, holds him over the chest of the mother, and lets the little dog go. He lands with a soft thud on his mother, then rolls to the ground. The mother gives a surprised yelp and jumps up. The nursing pups whine as nipples are yanked from their mouths. The puppy that was dropped pumps his tiny feet furiously in the air. Then he rights himself. The mother licks him clean.

Soon, all five of the puppies lay down in the leaves and the nursing resumes.

Devlin shakes his head again. *Stupid dog.*

He descends from his perch and fills in the hole, from the street side, by gathering rocks, dirt, and litter. Then he gathers up the apples and the day's meager plunder and heads home.

# Chapter 14

## *Ephemeral Stream*

The moment Amanda steps off the porch, she starts to feel disoriented. Swallowing hard, she makes her way across the rolling lawn. Her lamp casts a faint halo. She can see a few feet ahead but can't see much beyond the glow. Ruts crisscross the landscape. She follows a cart path. Piles of sticks and garbage have been deposited by the flood. She finds herself veering slightly to the left, then to the right. The silhouette of the barn lies ahead, but why does it take her so long to make the walk? She may be off course.

She sees other people in the yard, but they have no interest in talking with her. Eventually, a woman, close to her own age, notices her and approaches. "Are you okay?"

Amanda nods. "I think so. I'm trying to get to the barn."

The woman gives a sympathetic look. "It can be confusing here in the dark. And the landscape has changed. I can walk with you if you'd like."

"Yes. Thank you."

They see another washed-out rut in front of them. This one is three feet deep with rubble in the bottom. There's a section of roof lying nearby, shingles still attached.

"Let's try to the left," the woman says. "I think we can get around the ditch over there."

They walk in silence for a minute. They are able to skirt the wash-out, but they must climb over other ruts and obstacles.

"By the way, my name is Amanda. What's yours?"

But just then the path grows slippery. Her companion doesn't answer because they both slide on the mud. In a moment, they are able to steady themselves.

"It's almost like someone tried to build a moat around the barn," Amanda quips. "But the water has retreated, and this mess is left."

"It never stays." The woman says. She looks directly at Amanda as she speaks.

"Do you mean the water?"

"Yes. It's ephemeral. Transient. It seldom comes through here, and when it does, it rearranges. It deposits. Then it's gone."

They again walk in silence, until Amanda asks, "How long have you been here?"

The woman is silent for a moment. "I'm not sure. A good while, I suppose. I came the same way most people do. From the river. Caught in a torrent."

"Were there a lot of people here when you arrived?"

"Dozens. Probably more."

They finally reach the barn. Amanda asks her new friend to come inside. But she politely declines. "Why are you going inside?"

"I was given a job to do. A cleanup. Of sorts."

"I see," the woman looks at the barn door. Then the latch. "Well, that tells me something. Something about you."

"It does?"

The woman bites her lip, then speaks. "Madam offers wise counsel. I've learned that much. She sees something in you. She knows what needs to be..." her voice trails off.

Amanda waits for her to finish. Grows impatient. "What?"

She avoids Amanda's gaze. "Addressed, if that's the right word. Maybe resolved. That's between you and her. She understands when people need to be strong. Do you feel strong enough to go in there?"

"I think I do. I hope so."

"Well then, I wish you well." Abruptly, she turns and walks away.

Amanda frowns, then turns toward the barn door. The lift latch is black iron. It looks unnecessarily thick and heavy. With great effort, she pulls the black bar up from its catch, pushes the door open, and steps inside.

# Chapter 15

## *Return Meeting*


Tobacco-chewing men lean silently against the front wall of The Rose Point Pub. They look up and down the street. Occasionally they expectorate in the direction of a spittoon that hasn't been cleaned in weeks.

A rumble of voices, low and deep, spills from the pub each time someone opens the door. It's a hissing waterfall of voices.

The Rose Point is always busy on a Friday evening. There is pay to spend and workers in need of a friendly ear.

Footsteps approach down a path littered with the butt-ends of hand-rolled cigarettes. The men leaning against the building look up, see a man they don't recognize, then look away indifferently.

The door opens again, and into the hiss and smoke of the pub wanders Jeb Thomas, fresh off an all-day train from Buffalo. His tired eyes scan the crowd for a familiar face. The man he is looking for is seated at a back table.


Devlin Richard's glass is empty. The waitresses aren't keen to visit a dark corner occupied by a man with a crusty facial scar.

Jeb nods to Devlin from across the room. Stops at the bar then heads to the back table, holding two beers.

"My God," Jeb says in genuine surprise when he sees Devlin up close. "What happened to your face?"

Devlin leans over his candle and smiles. "Same thing that's going to happen to yours if you're wasting my time."

Jeb pulls out a chair and sits. His fear of Devlin has waned. He just wants to complete their business.


Devlin, for his part, had hoped to never see Jeb again. But displeasure can be overlooked if there's money to be made.

"You know," Devlin says to Jeb, "I wasn't sure if I'd see you. I know that the cops have a habit of tossing you in jail. Not just here. All around the country apparently."

Jeb laughs, gingerly flicking drips of foam from the side of his mug. "Yeah, well, you know how it is. Some people love me, and a lot of people don't. It's part of the business."

"A wise man knows how to stay low," Devlin counters. "Myself? I've never seen the inside of a jail. Doubt I ever will."

Jeb studies Devlin's new scar. There is no doubt in his mind the man knows how to find his way out of a tough scrape. "Look, let's get down to business, shall we? Are there any new details on the box?"

Devlin stares at him for several seconds before responding. "I'm going to tell you this in confidence. And that's only because I need your help to make the final connections. And if you ever try to cut me out of this deal, so help me, Mr. Thomas, I'll kill ya. I'll hunt you down like a damn dog."

"And I will do the same to you, if the shoe ends up on the other foot, Mr. Richards. You can count on that."

Devlin gives him a skeptical look, then files his report: He knows roughly where the box is, but he's not able to retrieve it. "I'm quite certain they're not keeping it in the Morgans' house," he says. "I think they've given it to a friend for safekeeping. I don't know where, but I think it's somewhere in the same neighborhood."

Jeb nods.

"So, I'm looking to you to come up with a plan to find out where it is. Maybe through the girl. When is she getting here?"

"I'm not 100 percent sure that she is."

"What?" Devlin sits back in his chair. He holds his hands up. "You're joking, right?"

"No. But I am playing the odds. This is a woman who has nothing to her name right now. Seriously, not one goddamn thing. So, where else would she go? My guess is she comes back here where she knows at least a few people and where she has some items that belong to her. That includes the box and an old steam carriage she previously abandoned. That's my prediction. She'll be back in Boston soon."

"Well, that's pretty damn vague. And what happens if she does come back? What then?"

"We'll be watching," Jeb smiles. "She'll certainly be looking for that box as soon as she arrives."

It was starting to make sense to Devlin. He could be closer to the prize than he realized. But the timing is risky. He takes a big swig of his beer. "Diamonds, big as your nuts, in that box. Isn't that what the sailor said?"

"He did, indeed," Jeb grins. "But the whole thing is still like playing the numbers, you know? We can't be sure we'll win. We also don't really know for sure about the size of those diamonds, assuming they even exist. We won't know until we have them in our hands."

# Chapter 16

## *It Follows*

Amanda sets the buckets and the lantern on the floor of the barn, then reaches to close the door. She wants no prying eyes.

*I can't believe I'm doing this.*

But she doesn't really know what to believe – because she has no idea what to expect.

What she does know is she wants to tackle this task to stay in Mrs. Lethe's good graces. It may help her find a way home.

Amanda looks toward the dark end of the barn. At first, she doesn't see anything at all. She swings the lantern to the left, then to the right. Nothing is visible. The barn seems empty, save for some bales of hay. As she walks toward the middle of the space, she finds herself passing a row of empty horse stalls. When she looks again, she sees something incongruous. The back of the stalls are lined with books. Fat scrapbooks, specifically, and they are neatly arranged on shelves. Each stall seems to have a number and several types of bound volumes.

She stops to look, hoping to understand, but she hears low breathing. It comes from a space a few feet beyond where the stalls end. Ignoring the books, she walks toward the sound.

Holding her lantern high, she tentatively approaches the place where the sound emanates. What she sees shocks her.

A pair of eyes reflect the lamp light. Slightly yellow. It's a strange and angry glow.

Then she sees more. She stands tall as she can. She's not sure if this is a man, a beast, or something in between. But she will be brave.

"Why are you naked?" she asks.

Howling laughter in response. Then hissing words. "Why are you not?"

She traverses in front of him. Keeping her distance. He looks straight ahead, avoiding her gaze. He seems formidable. Yet vulnerable too. At least he seems open and unprotected – tied here in the barn.

She reverses and walks back to his front. He seems to avoid her gaze, then he suddenly jerks his head, catching her eye. She jumps. He laughs.

Taking a deep breath, she tries to show determination by stoically holding his gaze for several moments. But the connection grows awkward and she looks away. Gaap laughs again.

"Mrs. Lethe was right," Amanda whispers. "I don't know who you are. I thought I might. But, no, I've never seen you before."

"That's strange," he says with heavy breath. "I feel like we've had many encounters. Perhaps you don't recognize me."

She holds the lamp high and studies him again. But she makes no connection. No admission.

"You shouldn't be here," she says. "Neither of us should be here."

He responds with a half-laugh, half-roar. The sound is low and guttural and echoes oddly off the beams of the barn. "No, no, we should not. And yet, here we are, both of us. What fun, no?"

"I'm not even sure what I'm supposed to do." Amanda looks around. She spies farm tools hanging on a wall.

"Don't you know? You came unprepared? It's my understanding that you're supposed to, I don't know, clean me up and then somehow vanquish me. Should be a straightforward effort. At least the cleaning part. Shall we get started?"

He howls again with laughter, flexing his muscles and standing straight. In that moment, Amanda realizes he is quite larger than she thought. There is much more to him. She doesn't think she can face this. For the first time, she feels threatened, even though he is bound.

She swallows hard. "This is absurd. I'm not able to deal with you. So, you know what? I'll just leave you. I'll let someone else pick up this burden."

His continued smile and unblinking eyes are unsettling.

"Ahh, yes," Gaap replies. "Not dealing with your burden. Our burden. That's so typical. How has that worked out for you so far? Oh, yes, dear Amanda, let's not make any new attempts to resolve what you find here. Best to leave things as they are." Then he snarls.

The ties on his hands suddenly look inadequate. Amanda backs away. If he is indeed a threat, he seems too large a challenge for one woman to deal with. "How do you know my name?" She demands. Then she looks toward the door.

"Thinking of running, Amanda? Again?"

She does run to the door. She tugs at it, but finds it locked. The other exits are locked too. She curses the woman who helped her find the barn. Her guide must have had some other motive in mind. And now she's trapped.

Amanda looks at the floor. She takes a deep breath and digs to find the inner strength she will need to continue.

With a shaky but renewed purpose, she walks back to face Gaap. She holds the lamp nearer his face and forces a tone of confidence into her voice.

"Tell me. Who are you?"

He laughs. "Someone from whom you have never been able to run."

She does not take the bait. Instead, she walks closer. "You never answered my first question." She walks forward. Looks him in the eyes. "Why are you naked?"

He scoffs. Shakes his head. "Sometimes it just happens. Aren't we lucky?"

"And sometimes you get exposed for who you are." She leans in. "No, I don't know you. Not personally. Not by name. But I think maybe, just maybe, I do know something of you."

He squints and tips his head to the side. "Ah. Yes."

"Yes, you have followed me," Amanda continues.

"Oh, I have long followed. A lifetime. You have been good at... avoiding." He looks her in the eyes. "Or failing to challenge. Or failing to vanquish. I'll leave it to you to find the right words. But you ignored and allowed me to follow. You let me grow."

There is an element of seduction in his gaze, but it turns her cold. "Why would I not avoid you? Look at you. Nothing to..."

"Nothing to be afraid of? Then why are you afraid? Why do you stand back? Why not just untie me? We'll sit. Chat a bit. Reminisce."

This time, it's Amanda who scoffs. "I am not afraid of you at all. She walks back to the wall. She makes a closer examination of the tools.

"Oh, I don't mean you're genuinely scared of me, dear. You're just scared of what I bring. Scared of what happens in my wake. Most people aren't even aware of something like me. I'm simply baggage. But to you?" He drops his head, then looks up at her slyly. "Perhaps, I'm a catalyst of sorts?"

Amanda keeps her back turned. She runs her fingers over a shovel. Then a pitchfork. "Sounds like it's best to avoid you altogether then. No?"

"Oh, I suppose it might be. But then, that would bring us back to where we are right now. With you running away yet again, eh? That's always been what you do. I've seen it. I know it well."

She pulls the pitchfork from the wall and turns around, prongs facing out. Gaap does not seem concerned. He continues his questioning. "You ran away from Montana, right? That's just the most recent. Away from Boston too? And before that, how many other places, dear? Boston to Cape Cod? From the Cape back to Boston? You leave friends in your wake. Men. Memories. You certainly do tend to run, don't you?" He gives a long howling laugh. Amanda feels a chill at the base of her neck.

"How do you know so much about…"

"About you? Oh, let's continue. What about as a child? Did you ever have a time when you weren't coming and going? Mother uninvolved. Shuffled from one relative to another, depending on their mood or yours. Never satisfied in one place, were you? Prone to dividing and changing the very nature of every house where you landed. That was you, no? Even when you lived with the Morgans, who so kindly took you in. You ended up dividing."

Gaap looks at her. Amanda looks back. "I did nothing to divide."

"Of course not. Perfectly innocent, weren't you? Fine, let's look elsewhere. How many men? Let's start with young Frank, back in grade school! Do you have any memory of him? He only wanted to sit with you. And as soon as he did, you moved on. You sat with others. So many young men, just like Frank. You always move on. Can we even remember all the names? Let's try."

Amanda walks forward, iron prongs pointed at the center of his shit-stained chest. "Enough!" she demands.

"Or what, dear? You want to kill me? Then do it. That fixes nothing. The problem remains even without me. It's in you. The puzzle you created is your own."

But she hesitates to stab him. She feels the need to explain.

"I just withdrew. I left bad situations. That's not running. It's being practical. Judicious."

Gaap raises his eyebrows. Nods. "I see. Well, that's different then. As long as all the withdrawing has helped you find your way, and find happiness, that's good! So, have you found that?" He lets the comment hang in the air for several seconds. Then he laughs, full and loud, like his voice has traveled through a megaphone. Amanda is certain he can be heard well out into the yard.

"You wicked thing," she shouts. "You know nothing of my happiness."

The pitchfork still does not seem to worry him. "I only know that whatever you think you're facing here – is a problem of your own making. A situation you avoided for too long." His voice drops to a low hiss. "It follows."

He raises his eyebrows. Offers a satisfied nod. "All your choices. All your bad turns. They do follow you."

Amanda closes her eyes. "I don't know what to do with you."

"Does it matter? Let's be done with running, you and I. We're washed into the gutter now. This sad swamp. And that overflowing bend in the river that pushed you here? You've drifted into a vast nothingness, and that gives you little else to run from. This can be the final place where you can stay. Where we stay, you and I, with all our burdens. So why not just give in? Yes, that's it. Just give in to it, dear. Come. Join me here. Bring over that soap and water. Let's pretend you can clean up this mess. We'll have fun, you and I. We'll accept our fates and go out in all our naked, zealous glory."

Gritting her teeth, she does pick up the water bucket. She empties it, dousing him full-on in the face. It surprises him and he shrieks at the cold, then spits as the water trickles down his nose and mouth.

"You bitch!" he shouts.

"I don't think you can hurt me after all," Amanda says as she plunges the sponge into the other soapy bucket and starts to scrub his left side where the largest of the pig shit stains is located. He squirms and bucks and swears at her, but she continues her work, scrubbing as hard as she can. She's angry at him. Angry at herself and her situation. Angry at everything that has transpired since she ran from Wayne and their farmhouse.

Then she turns and plunges the sponge back into the water and starts again, this time on his right side.

The filthy curses spilling from his mouth grow worse. He calls her terrible words – some in languages she's never heard before. He challenges everything, from her birth legitimacy to the profession of her mother. Still, Amanda scrubs on.

Then she picks up the soapy bucket and uses what's left to splash him again. He looks less threatening now. And he's fairly clean.

Gaap shakes the water from his face. He growls, then forces a smile. "Now wasn't that fun. But it seems like you hate me. Do you? Do you hate all of us? All men?"

Amanda closes her eyes.

Images of the past ten weeks swirl through her mind. Wayne's nastiness that drove her to start this journey back in June. Her perilous escapes since then. Jeb's secret violent streak. Ephraim's hormone-fueled pursuit. All of it has lit a fire inside her, to the point where she wants to lash out and fight back.

This terrible person, this thing in front of her, seems like a perfect and most deserving target for her wrath.

She looks back to the wall of the barn, where the other farm implements hang. Saws. Scythes. A wagon jack and a heavy metal bar. She closes her eyes. She feels a disconcerting shiver over what she might be tempted to do. She knows Gaap saw her look.

And that's when something else enters her head. And that thought keeps her from becoming too extreme, though he certainly deserves it.

The thought which percolates up from deep inside is this – she's also seen remarkable goodness in some men. There was Elmer, who helped her on the Cape Cod beach. The old man even gave her his steam wagon so she could be free.

There was Jonathan Morgan and his patient paternal respect and assistance.

61

And then there was Corporal Zandor, a man who rescued her on the plains and who was always a perfect gentleman.

And what of Victor Marius? She never had the chance to meet him. She never will. But how can she ever forget him and the thoughtful things he wrote? Victor seemed driven. Conflicted. Ambitious. Respectful of all. She feels like she has seen deep into Victor's soul, and she likes the little bit she managed to discover there. And even Victor seemed conflicted and lost before he went down on that ship.

In contrast, this beast she faces now is not at all a humble and honest human.

He's a byproduct. He's a presence that should never have been ignored.

"No," Amanda responds. "I'm not a hater of men, or women or anyone." She looks him in the eyes. "Well, maybe just you. I should be done with you."

"And you think you can just kill me?" He looks directly back at her.

She grabs his chin and looks him directly in the eyes. "Tell me, Gaap, if that's your real name, do you deserve it?"

He doesn't respond. Amanda's gaze is drawn back to the wall of tools. "Well? Do you?"

"I've never hurt anyone," he claims. "Not physically. Can you say the same?"

"Stop turning this back toward me!"

"It's very much about you. Make your choice. I have confidence you will always make the wrong one. And, when you do, again, I will be waiting."

Her face goes pale. Her fists clench. She retrieves her pitchfork from the floor.

He remains relentless. "How did you end up in the gutters, Amanda? How do any of us end up here? This river valley? It's the biggest gutter in the country, and this is where you ended up. You can't change who you are."

Amanda takes a stance and prepares to throw the fork like a spear. She finally sees shock and trepidation in Gaap's eyes. "Well, I'm surprised! I didn't think you would do…" But before he can finish, Amanda's arm moves fast and the pitchfork flies toward him. Those are the last words out of his mouth. The forks drive deep. Gaap's body disintegrates like smoke. The tool, seemingly unbloodied, flies through the spot where his body stood, over the gate where he was tied. Then it clatters to the floor.

Amanda stands alone and with her mouth open for several moments. She looks at the empty space. Her arms drop to her sides, fists clenched. But the threat and the baggage that came with her task to clean things up – it all seems to be vanquished. She turns her head to the side, squinting in anger. But then a smile slowly comes to her lips. She kicks the empty bucket from her path and heads toward the door. She finds it unlatched now. Outside, her guide awaits, lamp still burning.

"Did you find what you needed to find?" The woman asks.

"We're done here," Amanda says as she steps past. She walks on without her escort. "He can go to hell, and so can you for bringing me here."

# Chapter 17

## *Training Days*

Victor isn't sure what to expect when he reports for his first day as a police trainee. But as the day goes on, he realizes he expected more than what he receives. The biggest surprise is what the department doesn't bother to teach him.

The first day is just a classroom session. One blackboard. One instructor. There is no book to read. No stories or advice from other officers. They don't even offer little skits to show the best way to approach an angry citizen or a weapon-toting criminal. Most of the lessons are about how to fill out paperwork, how to ask questions, and the importance of writing everything down in a small notebook. The other bit of advice? If he's ever in a shootout, aim for the dead center of the chest.

When Victor arrives at the police station the following day, he learns he will be assigned to a partner. Watching how that partner conducts himself while walking patrol is, apparently, the main way he will learn his police duties.

Then, the very next speaker tells the group that manpower is in short supply, and several of the new officers, including Victor, would not actually have a partner on some days.

In the late morning, they spend considerable time discussing which people or groups in the city are considered friends of the police, and which are not. Always take care of our friends first, the group is told.

In the afternoon, a new instructor talks about the importance of staying in shape. He encourages all of them to routinely visit one of the two police gyms maintained by the city. But by the looks of some of the older officers, Victor can tell attendance at the gyms is optional.

When Victor returns the next morning, each trainee is issued a gun and a badge. They are told they must purchase their own uniforms from a little shop next door to the main police station. The shop turns out to be owned by the wife of the commander of the station.

Thankfully, Victor finds he does not have to walk his beat alone on his very first day in uniform. He's assigned to an older partner, Corporal Ned Tucker, who at first scoffs at the idea Victor is only working part time.

"What the hell! Are you kidding me? They expect me to babysit a new guy who's not even planning to be here every day?"

Tucker carries on and complains enough that Victor eventually turns to him and says, "If this isn't going to work for you, then why don't we go in, tell the captain he made a mistake, and that both of us want to be assigned to someone else?"

The older cop blinks. Then laughs. "You've got some stones, lad. I'll give you that." And for the rest of the day, the two get along fairly well.

Victor's biggest surprise comes later in the afternoon. He learns the city's ongoing law enforcement efforts largely fall under the influence of politicians. "Anyone from the mayor's office or any of the city councilmen ask you to do something," Tucker says, "you just do it. Understand? Except for Seth Anderson. Fuck that guy."

"What do you mean?"

"I mean the current Mayor has been good to the police. He looks out for us, unlike the previous two. They were pricks. So, when he looks out for us, we look out for him. He gave us a bump in pay. Just remember, it's good to have a top-level friend, so if any requests come out of his office, and if they trickle down to you, just make damn sure to handle them." He leans forward. "If you don't, I don't think you want to be the one trying to explain to your fellow officers why no one gets a raise next year."

"I guess not."

"I didn't think so. But as for Anderson, he always votes against the Mayor, and he voted against the most recent police budget. We all hate him. If you see him on fire, don't even bother to piss on him."

"I see."

"So, that's it. If the mayor or one of the other councilmen asks you to chase folks off a street corner? You do it. If they ask you to kick a little tail on election day to keep people away from the polls? You do it.

Understand? You walk that line like the rest of us, and you'll do fine here."

Victor doesn't respond.

Corporal Tucker changes the subject. "You know, this force isn't as old as you'd think. Not as old as New York and other cities. We only were founded in 1855. That's just 36 years ago."

"Wait," says Victor, "You're telling me there were no cops in the city before 1855?"

"Well, there were guards and such. Citizen day patrols. And before that, we had the lamplighters. City gave them lamplighters a little extra so they'd keep watch on things overnight. There were also private constables and volunteer groups. Guess that worked for years. But as the city grew, and once the Irish started coming in, the Germans too, well, they all made a mess of things."

"I see." Victor could tell Corporal Tucker enjoyed telling this history, even as he used a broad brush.

"They'll be assigning you to a ward, and then you just walk the streets of that ward. Those are your people. You take care of them. Some of 'em anyway. The local councilman? You take care of him too. He'll make sure people look out for you and treat you well. You want a free lunch while you're working? Free drink after? Nice little Christmas gift? That will all come. You play nice, you stay on the right side of the right people. Well, word gets around. Even the shopkeepers will be nice if they like you. By the way, I don't know where you'll be assigned, but if you're working over by the garment district, keep an eye out for union activity. Business owners hate that shit. Drives the costs up for the mill owners and haberdashers. They'll pay you good money if you can tell them about any union stuff you see. If you find a union poster on a wall, tear it off and bring it to a mill office. Great way to make a few extra coins."

The lessons continue for the next two days. Victor watches Corporal Tucker in action. Four arrests. One quiet pay-off in the back of a lawyer's office. On the fifth day, Victor reports for duty and is told he will be on his own from that point. Not enough officers to keep doubling up. He receives a new assignment.

"I don't feel like I'm ready for this," he tells his partner.

"Ahh, you'll be fine. And one more thing," Tucker says before they part ways. "Don't be afraid to take your nightstick out of your belt. Just hold it in your hand while you're walking the street. Be nice, but let the punks know you're out there and that you mean business."

# Chapter 18

## *Morning After*

As Amanda walks back to the huge house, she sees no one. No workers in the fields. No Mrs. Lethe. No housekeepers.

The sky is a bit lighter to the east, with hints of red. She feels gratitude for the coming dawn but doesn't remember the rest of the night passing once she left the barn.

She heads through the front door and traverses the long hallway. In the distance, she hears dishes clattering. Instinctively, she heads toward the kitchen.

She finds three women there, tending the stoves and arranging the dishes. Amanda does not recognize any of them. It's as if a new crew has arrived and settled into the duties. They pay her no mind.

There is a kettle boiling on the stove. Loose tea sits in a glass jar beside a stack of cups. Ignoring etiquette, Amanda takes a handful of tea, throws the ground leaves directly into a cup, and roughly adds the hot water. Warming her hands on the thin bone china, she takes a sip then exits the kitchen through a screen door. Along the side of the building, she finds an empty garden. A curved stone bench stands beneath a rose trellis. That's where she chooses to sit.

The tea is splendid. Each time the cup rises to her lips, she sees steam lift and curl against the soft dawn light.

Amanda sits quietly for some time, until the tea is nearly gone. What remains has grown quite cold. As the sky brightens, birds arrive and splash at a nearby bath.

This bench… it's a soothing place. She's come to realize most of this complex of buildings, save the foreboding barn, has a soothing feel. It invites a visitor to linger. It bestows a reward for inertia.

A bright Cardinal hops from the bath to the far end of her bench. Amanda looks at him. He looks back.

"Okay, little bird, where do I go now? You could be anywhere, and yet you're here. Is that a good thing? Will you stay?" The bird cocks its head. Then it flies away. She looks after it, following its path until it disappears across a field.

Amanda sits until it's fully light. Until the dew disappears from the grass. Eventually the kitchen door bangs, and she sees Mrs. Lethe walking toward her through the garden.

# Chapter 19

## *Limited Options*

Devlin is 10 feet down a dark alley, standing near the shadows and staring at a young woman. Her face is a mass of smudged eye makeup. Unbrushed hair and threadbare clothes. She's looking to tap into whatever business he might offer her for the evening, but he's not biting. At least not in the way she is expecting.

Devlin takes a handful of coins from his pocket, then holds one up for her to see. It's a silver dime. "Let's just talk," he says. "Is that alright?"

"Sure," she responds, tugging at her worn blouse. "Lots of guys just want to talk."

Devlin presses the dime into her hand. She grasps it eagerly.

"I recognized you when I saw you. You were part of the old house, right? The one in the warehouse district?"

She nods.

"You were there right up until the end, no? When things got shot up and everything went to hell?"

She nods again, and he gives her another dime.

"In fact, when Irene left, a group of girls went with her, you were one of those girls, right?"

She nods again, and takes a third dime. But then she looks up, in a bit of a panic. "You... you're him. Aren't you? The one who sprayed the place with bullets." She takes a step back. "Or at least you were there that night."

Devlin shrugs. "I'm just someone who is trying to understand things. Same as you. And by the way, I don't like the term spray. I shoot deliberately. I hit my targets."

The young woman closes her hand around the coins and turns away. Devlin reaches, arm curving around in front of her face. He lets her see a small gold coin. She reaches for it, but he pulls his hand back.

As she turns to face him, Devlin can see she's biting her lip.

"You want?"

She nods.

"Then you tell. Where is she?"

"Who?"

"For fuck's sake, stop playing dumb. You left with Irene. I just want to know where she is."

"I... I don't know. We aren't together anymore. None of us."

"Maybe not. But you can tell me where she went. Let's start with when she first left. Maybe you even know where she is now? Coin is coin, dear. Gold is gold."

He sees her bite a fingernail. Something in her face and movements makes him realize she may be even younger than he thought. Mid-teens. Looking older because of makeup. Looking older because she's been surviving on her own – the only way she can.

"How about," he holds up the gold coin, "you just tell me the first place she went after that night, and I give you this gold coin? And if you tell me where she is now, I'll buy you something to eat too!"

He can see the girl's conflicted look. But he senses he has turned her. Within a few seconds, she takes the coin. Then she picks up a stick and draws some lines in the dirt, showing him a grid of streets. She points to a long cul-de-sac where their group first retreated.

"We stayed there for several days. But things turned ugly. Too many strangers. Irene couldn't set up shop there, and we all started fighting. The girls drifted away. I did too."

"Just working the streets now? Alone?"

She blushes. Nods. Looks away.

What happened from there?

"Irene eventually moved. Heard she went to a small house out by Huntington Avenue Grounds. Shadow of the ballpark."

"Which one?"

"I don't know. I don't know fuck-all about sports. I just heard it was a ball park." Tears form in her eyes. "Come on, didn't I give you what you asked for?"

Devlin nods. "You did. Here's the gold. And here are two more dimes. Get yourself something for dinner."

On the way home, he stops in to see Jeb, who has found a room to rent. House of an old widow who seems content to leave him alone. They sit on a back balcony where they plan a bit, and argue a bit, about where Amanda might be, and whether she will ever come looking for her lost puzzle box. Eventually they come up with a foundation of a plan.

"I have kids who work incredibly cheap. Just watching. I even have some eyes over at the train station. They'll pass information along quickly," says Jeb. "If she comes through there, we'll know."

# Chapter 20

## *The Beat*

A dark blue police uniform can make the sun's rays feel even hotter. On this sunny day, it's hot enough to send Victor toward the shady side of the street.

A bridge takes him across a small but active waterway known as Stony Brook. Unlike other brooks in Boston, this one drains a relatively small area. It's a clean spring-fed water source with a good steady stream, which is why a few breweries eventually sprouted up along its banks. Highland Spring, Burkhardt Brewing, and Burton.

A successful working-class neighborhood has also evolved near these buildings. Pockets of German and Irish immigrants dot the streets.

Victor's part-time assignment is to walk this neighborhood. After a few days, he's decided this isn't such a bad way to spend his time. The problems here are minimal. A few drunks. An occasional fight. A potential pickpocket that he was able to chase off fairly quickly. All in all, he feels at ease here. He could have been assigned to a much worse neighborhood.

Victor nods to a youth fishing from the bank of the brook.

Strolling on, he sees a few men pressing their weight down on a log that's wedged over a rock and under the bed of a wagon. They're trying to raise a broken wheel off the ground so it can be replaced. The bed is filled with wood. The men are obviously hoping to avoid unloading it, but they are struggling against the weight. Victor joins them and leans hard on the end of the log. That extra effort helps raise the wagon a few more inches. In a matter of minutes, the wheel exchange is complete, and they thank him for lending his weight.

That's pretty much how he spends his first few days on the job. Walking. Watching. Making polite chat with the locals and helping where he can. One thing he quickly learns is that a police officer doesn't necessarily need to be anywhere, other than in their assigned neighborhood. Their job is mostly to be seen. People like to know that some sort of protection is nearby.

Because this is a populated area, there was a haphazard competition among the city's electric companies to reach this area. Victor can tell, based on the types of wires and insulators, which companies have run wires to specific blocks.

When there's little else for him to do, he walks the sidewalks and looks up at the utility poles, making a mental note of how many overhead wires they carry, and whether the installation looks good or slipshod.

By the time his shift ends, one particular circuit has caught Victor's attention. The wires look thin and cheap. The connections seem sloppy and fat with black tape. He decides to follow those wires and finds they lead to a small side creek that connects to Stony Brook. And there he discovers the remains of what must have been an old water-powered grist mill. The wooden part of the mill is long gone, but someone has used the old stone foundation to install a metal paddlewheel connected to a generator.

The equipment is covered by a temporary shed roof supported by pieces of broken utility poles lashed into place. It's cheap and shoddy-looking. He walks closer.

The gears whir, and the electricity, what little there is of it, crackles. Victor watches in wonder, realizing this may be one of the most primitive and haphazard generator installations he's ever seen. With the demand for electricity booming, every businessman in Boston is trying to get into the power-generation business. Inspections are supposed to take place, but the city is understaffed and things like this sometimes run unchecked.

He shakes his head. When his next shift starts in two days, he will follow the wires in the other direction. Whoever was duped into becoming a customer of this slapdash system, he wants to see if the work at the other end, at their homes and businesses, looks as dicey as the powerplant. If so, he may elect to warn those places that it's probably time for them to switch to a more competent provider.

After his shift, Victor stops by the police station, to remind the supervisor he won't be working the next morning.

"I'm heading to New York City on the train, first thing in the morning," Victor explains.

"Oh, yeah? What for?"

"Just a meeting. I'm working on a project. I know an engineer there." Victor doesn't mention Tesla because he's certain the other officer has never heard of him.

"Yeah? Well, have a nice trip. Keep in mind no one will be walking your beat while you're gone. See you when you get back."

# Chapter 21

## *Departure*

Amanda rises from her seat in the garden and looks toward the sun. Her conversation with Mrs. Lethe went well. They both understand it's time for Amanda to leave. She feels like this is a victory of sorts.

"I'm deeply grateful for your help," Amanda confides. "I don't know if I would have survived this ordeal if it had not been for your hospitality."

"Nonsense, my dear. It's me who should thank you. You helped us get rid of that intruder, whoever he was."

Amanda takes a breath. "But you certainly know he was only here because he followed me. If I had not come, he would not have arrived." She looks at the old woman and sees, in the morning light, just how old she seems.

Mrs. Lethe crinkles her eyes. "Believe me, you are not the first to draw such visitors along with you. You won't be the last. But you dealt with things admirably, my dear, and you should be proud."

Amanda considers the words, but doubts pride is the right emotion. "I felt more desperate than anything."

Mrs. Lethe purses her lips for a moment, then speaks. "You know, moments of desperation can be quite defining. If you have any strength at all, such moments are when you find it. But if strength is lacking, you may find nothing."

The matron of the manor slides forward in her chair. "Last night, quite likely, was a memorable one for you. Perhaps it even sparked great changes. You will know in time. It's the same in anyone's life."

She catches Amanda's eyes.

"Surely you can think of a day, not necessarily last night, but maybe just one day in your life when there was a choice to be made. You made the choice and likely never thought about it again. But the choice, in some small way, changed you."

Amanda nods.

"Each time you face a choice, any choice, it changes your route oh so slightly. Like a river slowly changing its course, it's a constant process. And to a person, their choices are like a chain. They connect you, from where you have been to where you are now. Perhaps that chain may be iron that binds you. But if you're lucky, it's more like a ring of flowers that captivates, yet holds no real weight. You can break it and head off toward new choices if you wish. But the reality is, no chain of any type can exist, but for the first link that formed when you started making choices. The selections you make ultimately are what guide you."

Amanda is silent for a minute. Then she looks up. "I don't even know what I chose last night."

"You chose to go on."

Amanda nods. "But what do I do now?"

The old matron takes her hand. "You do just that. You go on – to whatever your next choice is. And all the choices to come."

Amanda thanks Mrs. Lethe and hugs her. She knows it's time to leave, but she's not sure how. She takes a first step by walking inside to gather her meager belongings.

When she returns to the main hall, she finds Mrs. Lethe seated in the center of the room – in a grand chair. A similar empty chair sits beside her.

Amanda starts to approach, but she hears a door open to her right. She turns to look, and what she sees causes her to pause. An old man walks through the opening. In Amanda's eyes, he looks impossibly old. In fact, he might be the most ancient being she's ever seen.

He walks, slowly, toward the empty chair.

"My husband, Mr. Elohim, has arrived, my dear. Most people never see him. I'm so glad you will have this honor."

The old man doesn't speak. He slowly approaches, then sits, in the other place of honor. His hand slowly reaches over to hold Mrs. Lethe's hand. Their fingers entwine. A ring of fresh flowers encircles her wrist. With her other hand, Mrs. Lethe gestures toward the open door, and then to the fields and trees beyond.

Amanda closes her eyes and speaks. "There is nothing in that direction except the river. And the space in between is probably just mud now, since the overflow must have receded."

The couple just stares at her. Then the old man makes the same gesture. *Go*. The door is open. The world lies beyond. It is hers.

Amanda nods, turns, and walks toward the open air.

With little of her own to carry, she walks toward the path where she came in. It takes her some time to find the way.

Eventually she follows the thin trail on a slow descent toward the river. In about 30 minutes, she passes back through the boughs of red leaves – the same ones that marked the start of her journey. She sees no sign of another soul.

More than once, she considers turning around, but when she looks back, she can no longer see the domed building.

Tired and confused, she sits down to rest in a spot not far from where she first climbed up out of the water. She lies back, letting the sun warm her face. In a few minutes, she falls asleep.

When Amanda awakens, the light has changed. She has no idea how long she's been there. It looks like a new morning.

She stands and surveys the field. The red leaves near the entrance to the path are no longer visible. She does not even see the sign that points visitors toward Angel Falls.

Her head hurts. She rubs her eyes and she realizes her hands are muddy. So is her dress and her hair. She finds bruises and bloody scratches along her arms and on her temple. Even taking a breath hurts.

Off in the distance, she hears the chug of machinery, and with no other view of civilization to draw her in a different direction, she heads toward the noise.

She looks back once more and sees nothing but trees.

Amanda walks through slippery mud, hanging on branches to steady herself. It's exhausting. Eventually she finds a stick to use as a hiking staff.

The wild tributary that temporarily formed during the storm has indeed receded. She faces a formidable field of rubble and muck that she must cross. Somehow. The chugging sound she heard must have been a steamboat. But the ship is not on this drying tributary. It must be out in the main river.

She looks above the distant tree line and sees a hint of smoke on the horizon, probably from that ship's stacks. It's heading away from her.

The mud grows deeper. She changes her direction and eventually comes to a line of debris that appears to have been the high-water mark from the flood. There, she sees all manner of things piled up. At first, she's disheartened. The pile looks unsteady and difficult to climb. But as she approaches, her mood brightens. The rubble contains pieces of houses, plus old trunks, clothing, furniture, and more.

It's upsetting to see the destruction, but she realizes there may be things of value here. Searching the pile may provide a strange salvation for a woman who has been left with nothing.

After several minutes of opening old suitcases and looking through shattered wardrobes, she receives her first payoff. Deep in the pocket of a muddy suit, she finds a billfold containing four ten-dollar bills. With renewed energy, she continues her search. Within an hour, she's also found more dollars, a pocket watch, multiple coins, and a woman's brooch. She is able to pry open the drawer of a shattered desk and finds a pair of older gold coins, plus a silver hairbrush.

Amanda continues her sculching. She only finds a few more things of value, but believes she has acquired enough to buy her way home. She may even have scavenged enough to survive for a week or two when she's back in Boston.

One of the last things she finds hanging from a branch is a woman's mid-length cloth coat. It has mostly dried in the sun and appears to be only a little dirty. She puts it on and climbs past the edge of the trash patch. She manages to navigate through the messy field, and after walking for an hour, she finds a cart path. Following that, she comes to a road that shows signs of recent horse traffic. Eventually she is able to flag down a passing wagon that holds a young family. She tells her story of being lost in the flood, and they find space for her.

As she rides away, she looks back one last time, hoping still to catch a glimpse of something, anything, connected to Angel Falls. But she sees no dome. No path. Nothing.

Amanda stares in that direction until the wagon descends the far side of a hill.

The mother of the group calls back to her. "You asked about a train station. There's one in the next town. Do you want us to drop you there?"

"Yes, please," Amanda responds. "That would be grand."

# Chapter 22

## *Diary*

When Amanda reaches the train station, she asks about tickets and reviews the different routes she might take toward the East Coast.

Ticket in hand, she explores the town's main street while she waits. She stops by a jeweler and sells the watch, the brooch, and the hairbrush for about thirteen dollars. She knows they're worth more, but she takes what is offered.

Then she stops at a telegraph office and sends a message to Jonathan and Beverly Morgan. She asks specifically that both names appear on the envelope. She tells the Morgans she's returning to Boston, and she hopes to reclaim the steam car they've been storing in their carriage house. She tries to make the telegram sound more formal and businesslike by offering to pay a storage fee. That should appease Beverly's distrust.

The last thing she does is buy a bound notebook and a pencil from a store called Conner's Mercantile, directly across from the station.

Amanda's ticket will take her to Charleston, West Virginia, a destination she chose out of caution. She believes Jeb, if he's still bothering to look for her, will expect her to take a northern route.

Instead, she'll stay slightly south. From Charleston, she plans to head to Washington, D.C., then up through the eastern rail corridors to New York City.

She settles into her seat, watches the landscape roll past, then opens her new notebook. She begins to write. Amanda has never kept a diary before, but this seems like a good time to start. She was inspired by Victor Marius and the tale he told. She has her own fantastic tale now.

Before she escaped from her husband and Cape Cod, her life was quite ordinary. But there's so much to say now in this new journal. So many adventures to set down, and so much emotion to peel back, like an endless onion. She doesn't know if she'll ever share these words with anyone, but if she doesn't put a record of these experiences onto paper, it feels like she'll just burst.

The conductor walks the aisles and calls for tickets. It's been many weeks since she's legally ridden on any sort of transportation, so his call causes her a twinge of panic. But she remembers that she holds an actual pass now. With gritted teeth, she reaches into her bag and presents her official train ticket. The man inspects it, punches it, and moves on.

Amanda beams. It was a simple transaction, but it feels like a tiny step toward becoming a human being again. Less wild. More decorous and less adrift.

She licks the tip of her pencil, and writes about that feeling.

*My original plan was to get a ticket by legal means, which I managed to do. But if necessary, I knew I could resort to outright thievery. And if I had not found a little money along the way, a rougher method of survival was my back-up plan.*

*Should I ever find myself in such dire straits again, I do believe I've figured out how to endure. I believe I could pick a pocket. It's a simple matter of tripping myself as a man comes near, falling into his arms, and slipping my hand into his jacket as he helps to set me right again. I understand this is not the activity of a good, honest woman. But it's certainly the act of a survivor. If the past several weeks have taught me anything, it's that I know I can survive.*

# Chapter 23

## *On Watch*

The morning is cool. Jeb warms his hands on a cup of coffee. There's a corner shop where they discount the price by a penny if you bring your own mug, so he usually does.

He stands on a corner, looking up the street. At this angle he can watch the front of Jonathan and Beverly Morgan's home. This is where Jeb lost track of the puzzle box, so this is where he's hoping to pick it up again.

He's followed Jonathan a few times in recent days, and he knows the old man has a small but tight circle of friends. If Jonathon passed the box along to anyone else for safekeeping, it's likely to be one of those friends. So, he watches and waits. He's also paid a few newsboys and messengers to keep watch for him.

But Jeb has another reason to watch the house. There's also a chance Amanda will show up here, and that is something he doesn't want to miss.

Long slow sip of coffee. Bored sigh.

He looks at the sidewalk. Kicks at the grass growing between the bricks.

Jeb knows he must come up with a better plan than to just linger. And he has to... well... He simply *has* to get Amanda back. But timing is key. He can't pounce at first sight. Nor can he just casually run into her. She would pull back. She would want to avoid him.

No, he must wait for the right moment, He must find a time when, somehow, he can come to her aid. He can't be someone who stalks her. Instead, he needs to come off as a hero.

Meanwhile, he also has contacts at the train station. Some of those friends know what she looks like. If she comes back to Boston, he will hear about it fairly quickly.

Another long sip off coffee. Another sigh

This is a delicate balance. The timing must be perfect. But Jeb is pretty sure he can make it work.

# Chapter 24

## *Alive and Missing*

Charleston. Then Washington, DC. Now New York City.

Today, Amanda Grant has little interest in viewing the Manhattan skyline. She climbs down from her train, brushing sleep from her eyes and dust from her dress.

Having traveled all night, and much of the previous three days, she just follows the crowd, duckling-like, toward the main concourse of Grand Central Depot.

The sprawling terminal includes three adjacent railroad buildings that house trains for the Hudson River Railroad, the New York and Harlem Railroad, and the New York and New Haven railroads. She winds her way through all three. Amanda needs a cup of tea and a moment to collect her thoughts. So joins a short line of people waiting at a food counter.

If this was a normal trip, she would just change trains and be on her way. But she asked to be routed through New York for a specific purpose. She's going to spend several hours here. There's someone she wants to visit.

From the other direction, entering through the depot's central doors, comes Victor Marius. He too is weary, but not from travel. The previous day, he arrived in New York with his folder full of drawings. He had intended to be in the city for just a day, but he and his friend and mentor, Nickola Tesla, ended up poring over the schematics for the full day and night.

The pair came up with some interesting design ideas and tweaks to Victor's transmitter plan. But Victor paid the price in morning fatigue.

Now he ambles, unshaven, toward the ticket counter.

He rummages through his pockets. Finds some cash. Tucking the ticket into his sheaf of papers, he stops for a moment, noticing the food counter at the end of the hall. *Now that looks good.* There's a large copper coffee boiler on the front counter. Maybe he'll get a cup to wake himself up. He rummages through his pockets again, this time seeking change.

After buying her mug of tea, Amanda walks to a nearby table. As she sips the hot liquid, she studies a small city map, specifically looking for the neighborhood where Nikola Tesla is supposed to live. She knows the name of the man and roughly where he lives, thanks to entries in Victor's diary.

She has no idea that Victor, who she believes to be dead, is walking just feet away.

He finds a nickel deep in his pocket and orders a hot cup of coffee. The attendant pours it from the caldron, which looks large enough to serve as the boiler for a small locomotive. Victor sips the dark liquid slowly, turning to look for a seat. All the tables are occupied. He thinks about asking someone if they'd like to share, but suddenly sees an empty bench across the concourse. He trudges toward it, hoping the coffee will abate his fatigue.

An agent walks through the concourse, announcing the arrival of a train from Philadelphia. Somewhere deep in the station, there's a rumble and hiss from a big engine. It vibrates the whole building.

Amanda closes her eyes and absorbs the rising din. How in the world can she find one man in this huge city? While she has a rough idea of where Tesla lives, she doesn't know how many buildings are on those streets, nor how many apartments are in each building. For that matter, she doesn't even know what this man, Tesla, looks like.

Still, she has a steady resolve. She must find him. Taking her tea with her, she stands and walks toward the door.

Victor stands too, coffee half-consumed, intending to make his way back toward the train platform.

Suddenly, to his right, he hears a flutter of paper. He looks over and sees a folded map lying on the polished floor.

"Miss?" He walks over to pick up the map. By now, the woman is nearly to the door. "Miss? I think you dropped this!"

She turns and looks at him. Their eyes meet and Amanda smiles. "Why, thank you," she says. "That's very kind of you."

She takes the map, nods, and heads toward the door. Victor walks on toward his train.

# Chapter 25

## *Bouncing Ball*


There is a small post office across the street from Grand Central. Amanda, suddenly, has an idea. An idea so elegant in its simplicity that she wonders why she didn't think of it before.

She crosses the street, enters the post office, and approaches the man at the counter.

"May I ask you something?"

The man looks up from a green ledger. "Yes. I suppose so."

"Can you tell me if there's a post office in this neighborhood?" She points to a spot on the map.

The mailman thinks for a moment. "I believe there is. It's on this street corner right here. Serves the whole area."

"Do you think, if I went there and gave them a name, they might be able to tell me where a person lives?"

"No. That's not something we're allowed to do."

Amanda nods, half expecting this. "That's such a shame. I'm a relative of his and haven't seen him since I was a child," she lies. "I'm only in the city for one day, and I had hoped to look him up."

"You didn't come with his address?"

"I didn't expect to be here this long, but now it looks like I have to take a different train. I will be here for several hours. I thought that might give me time to make a visit."

"Can you call or send a telegram to a relative to get the address? You might hear back in just an hour or so. Well, that's assuming the other person lives close to a telegraph office."

"No. No, they don't. Oh, I guess we won't be able to meet. That's a shame." She musters the cutest smile she can manage and thanks him for his time.

"Wait. Who is he, exactly, the man you're looking for?"

"He's my uncle. My godfather actually. But my family moved away many years ago. It really would be fun to see him again. He's nearly retired now!"

The postman's eyes shift left and right. "Look. I'm not supposed to do this, but I do know someone who works at the office in that neighborhood. Let me write a quick note to him. I don't know what he might be able to do for you, and it will be up to him whether he helps you or not. But he might."

A half hour later, she arrives at that other post office, explaining that she needs to find Nikola Tesla. The clerk reads the note and passes it to a man in the back room, who emerges, smiling.

"I see my friend Russell at Central is being bad, encouraging me to break the rules for you."

"Oh, please, if you could find it in your heart."

He laughs. "The problem is, I don't know anyone by the name of Tesla. People come and go a lot, you know, so I guess he could be here. But I don't have a clue where."

Amanda looks dejected, but tries again.

"He is relatively new here, actually. And he's a scientist. Do you have any newcomer who's received a lot of correspondence recently from electrical companies?"

He shakes his head.

"All right then. Thanks anyway."

She's nearly to the door when the clerk calls out, "Wait, what kind of company? Can you name one of the companies who may have sent him something?"

"Yes. How about Westinghouse?"

His eyes brighten.

"Well, yes. Of course. There is a new gentleman, dark bushy mustache, heavy accent, who has received two fat letters from Westinghouse this week. I remember them because of their size, and because I thought that was a strange name for a company."

Amanda runs to him, grasping his hands.

"Yes. YES!"

He gives her the number for the building, and she thanks him profusely.

She arrives at an apartment building that's sheathed in gray stone, looking a bit like a fortress.

She steps into the dark hallway, finding a pair of girls there, one at the top of the stairs and one at the bottom. The girl at the top tosses the ball down the stairs, allowing it to bounce a few times before the other girl catches it. The game stops when they see that they have a spectator.

"Hello!" says the girl at the top stair.

"Hello," Amanda smiles. "That looks like a fun game."

"It's hard!" the older girl boasts. "You have to drop it just right to get three bounces. If you don't, you have to go to the bottom. That's the rule. I'm better at it, so I get to stay up here more than her."

"That's not true!" the girl at the bottom stair retorts, throwing the ball upward. "You just keep changing the rules."

"I do not!"

The argument escalates until Amanda interrupts. "Excuse me, but I wonder if you could help me?" She asks about Tesla, only to receive two blank stares. She doesn't know how to describe him, so she gives only a few sketchy details. His rough age. His mustache, though every man seems to have a mustache these days. And his accent.

"Wait!" one interrupts. "Do you mean the sausage man?"

"Your mom said not to call him that," her friend responds.

"Well, that's what you and I always call him, right?" She turns to Amanda. "His apartment always smells like sausages. Mom says that's because people from his country eat a lot of sausages and things like that."

"I see," Amanda watches the ball bounce down the stairs. "Well, I suppose that could be him."

They tell her a bit more, including details about his accent. She decides the sausage man could very well be the man she seeks.

"But he's not here right now. He went out a while ago. We saw him."

Amanda thanks them and helps chase the ball when it takes a bad bounce. The two girls argue about whether the latest bounce was fair, or whether there should be a do-over because Amanda was talking and the girls were distracted.

Amanda thanks them and slips outside to wait. She isn't sure what to do. She's so close now. It would be a shame to miss him. But she can't just park herself on the stoop for hours.

A few minutes later, the young girls emerge through the door and stand beside her, full of questions.

She asks their names. The girl with the light hair is Molly, and the one with the dark hair is Angela. With just a hint of an Italian accent, Angela looks to be the older of the two.

"Why do you want to see him?" Angela asks. "Is he your beau?"

Molly giggles.

"No. He just knows someone who I also know. I mean, in a way. That's all. I want to talk with him about something."

"Angela has a boyfriend too!"

"I do not."

"Do too," she taunts. "Jacob Myers!"

"What! I don't like him at all! Why you...." She chases Molly down the street, and they return a few moments later with a barrel hoop and two sticks. It's as if they've totally forgotten their argument. And so it goes for the next hour, with the two girls disagreeing, then distracting themselves with a new game, then returning to talk with Amanda again.

The hoop game in particular keeps them occupied. Amanda even takes a turn, helping roll it all the way to the corner. Finally, as they roll it back toward the steps, they see a thin mustachioed man walking from the other direction.

"Sausage man?" Amanda asks.

"Sausage man!" Molly shouts.

Amanda asks them to scoot away, saying she has important business, but they lurk nearby, trying to listen to the conversation.

Amanda waits on the first step, just high enough to look him in the eye.

"Are you Mr. Tesla?"

The man stops, looking up. He says nothing for several seconds, then asks, "Do I know you?"

"No, sir." She introduces herself as Amanda Grant. "We've never met. I... I'm just looking for information on a mutual friend. I mean, he *could* be mutual if you're who I think you are. … But I've never… I mean, that is…."

She laughs at herself. Why has she become so flustered? She blurts out Victor's name.

Tesla laughs too and confirms he is, indeed, the man she seeks. "And, yes, I know Victor. Very well. Why are you looking for him?" His thick accent hangs like fuzz on every word.

I… well, I found some things of his. Including a diary. I guess I just wanted to find out more about him."

"You read his diary? Oh my. I wonder if he would like that."

She laughs. "Yes, well, I've wondered too. But I think maybe he'd like to know he left something behind. Something that was found by someone. And read."

"Left behind where?"

"From a shipwreck."

"Ahh! The shipwreck. You mean you found it after Victor's wreck?"

She nods, explaining how the pieces of the Gossamer washed up on Cape Cod, and how the sandy beaches become scavenging grounds whenever shipwrecks happen.

Tesla invites Amanda inside. But she instead invites him to stroll to a small park at the end of the street. Angela and Molly tag along behind. Amanda asks the Croatian scientist about his work with Victor. What they did, and why Victor ended up on that boat, conducting his experiments.

"It's a shame that you weren't here earlier this morning. You could have asked him these questions yourself."

Amanda laughs, thinking he's joking.

"Yes, we had quite a nice meeting, Victor and I."

Amanda slows her steps, wondering if she's walking with a crazy person. Or maybe this Mr. Tesla misunderstood who she's talking about.

"What's the matter?" Tesla laughs. "You wouldn't want to meet him?"

She tries to smile. "Yes. Of course, I would. But I'm not sure how I might react. When I was growing up, my minister told me the living should not try to talk to the dead."

Tesla laughs, long and hard. Even the laugh sounds foreign to her. "The dead? Oh, my dear. I guess you don't know, do you?"

Amanda stares at him.

"Oh, but now this all makes sense," Tesla continues. "I once thought he was dead too. All of us did. But, no, he's very much alive, my dear. Victor Marius is alive and quite the survivor."

By the time they reach the center of the park, Amanda's knees are weak. Tesla takes her arm and they walk toward a bench. As she sits and stares at the ground, he tells her everything. The wreck. The rescue. Victor's lost work and research. His survival and road back to health. The story ends with Victor's visit with Tesla, just within the past few hours.

Amanda has questions – dozens of them, but they don't find their way to her lips. Instead, she finds herself just staring. She shakes her head.

"Ms. Grant? Are you all right?" he asks.

She swallows. "I… I guess I am." She brushes imagined wrinkles out of her skirt. "Yes, of course. And thank you so much for the information."

Tesla studies her with concern. "Victor… he means something to you apparently?"

She shrugs. "Maybe he does. But he's a man I've never met. I just read what he wrote. I liked the way he thought. Well… now I guess I should say I like the way he *thinks*. He has the same questions about everything as I do." She pulls the diary out of her skirt pocket. "And I guess I wanted to return this diary to his family, or a friend like you. To put him to rest, so to speak. But now…"

Amanda doesn't understand this rush of mixed feelings. Shock. Delight. Awe. Plus, there's a troubling sense of foreboding. Knowing Victor is alive changes everything she felt about him. Before, he was distant. Tragic. An enigma. But alive? Is he still that same person? Will he measure up to the myth? She's not sure how she feels.

"I'm afraid I don't know where any of his family members live," Tesla replies. "I know he has an old building in Boston he uses as a laboratory. He also uses it as his home. But can't tell you where that is exactly. If you like, you could leave the diary with me. I'm sure I'll see him again sometime."

She almost agrees. But now she doesn't want to part with it. She realizes it could be her ticket to meeting him someday, even if that takes years. What incredible satisfaction she'd feel if she was able to hand it to him! She rescued it from the sea and is returning it. She can only imagine his surprise.

Her thoughts are interrupted by Tesla's voice. She turns toward him to listen. "When we were walking here, you asked about what sorts of things he was working on the day the ship went down. Would you like to see?"

"Really?"

"Victor told me, when he was on that trip, he wrote in his journal every day, mostly about his radio project. Let's see what he wrote for those last days. I know he loved sketching out his thoughts. There might be some drawings." Tesla takes the diary and flips through it, until he finds some pencil sketches.

"I wasn't sure what those drawings were when I saw them," Amanda says.

Tesla points to parts of the illustrations and explains how radio waves are created, and how they can travel vast distances. He finds a few blank pages at the rear of the notebook and takes out a pen, adding his own drawing. He explains the device Victor developed that can make a short spark, which in turn sends a wave through the air. He tells her how he worked with Victor just last night, to suggest some improvements. "Something is created by these sparks. A pulse. We call it a radio wave. Other systems can detect that pulse, even miles away." Then he points to the center of the diagram. "But I can tell you this, Victor told me he won't build his next version in quite the same way. In this older design, it sometimes builds up an excess electrical charge —if the power generation and the spark continue for too long. Eventually that charge must go somewhere. Sometimes it dissipates that extra charge by sending a very dangerous arc through the air. It grounds itself on whatever it touches. That arc could shock people or maybe start a fire."

He also tells her how, because of the way these radio waves travel, they can be used to transmit messages. "You know about Morse code that's used in telegraph messages, right? That code can be used with wireless signals too. At least in theory. I like to think it could carry a voice someday too, just like a telephone. But that's a long way off."

Amanda's eyes glaze over. She isn't sure she understands all he's saying, but she thanks him for the explanation.

"So where will you go now?" Tesla asks.

"Back home, I think. Back to Boston."

"I wish I could help you find him. If I do see Victor again, I'll tell him about you. And I will tell him you have his journal."

Amanda smiles. "I can't say yet where I will be living. Oh, you have no idea at all how I might reach him?"

"I wish I did, my dear. His train left this morning. I only know he'll be somewhere back in your city. I know he's planning to continue his work with his old college professor. Meanwhile he said he's working as a police officer, though if his work on the electric lines picks up, he may follow that opportunity rather than continuing with the police. Oh, he's in such flux right now. Much like you, I suppose."

"I see."

"Another problem will be, if he does go back to electric line work, he could head out of town for months and months. In that case, I don't think you will find him at all."

Amanda nods. "Well, that is a challenge. But thank you. And if you do see him, please tell him to send me a letter. Boston general delivery." She gives him the address of the central Boston post office.

"Wait. I don't suppose you have access to a telephone?"

Amanda laughs. "Me? A telephone? Hardly. I could never afford that, and I don't know anyone who can."

"Pity," Tesla laments. "I recently had one installed. I could call you if I knew how to reach you." Then he laughs. "I really don't have many people I can call. Just Westinghouse, should he care to hear from me."

They part company, with Tesla heading back to his apartment and Amanda heading to the train station, and toward her very uncertain future.

She's not sure where those two girls went. Last time she saw them, they were chasing a pigeon.

# Chapter 26

## *The Run-down*

Walking his police beat for the third day, Victor finds his neighborhood to be fairly quiet. But the serenity doesn't last.

At one in the afternoon, he spots a teenage girl waving to him from a distance. She seems upset and keeps looking over her shoulder. Just as Victor starts jogging toward her, several other people come around the corner. They also start shouting and waving to him. They all point toward something he can't yet see.

Victor breaks into a run. When he reaches the group, everyone starts talking at once. He rounds the corner and can instantly see what's going on. A man lies bleeding in the street. There's a gash on his head and blood on the cobblestones. A brick lays a couple of feet from his body.

"That poor man!" says a woman. "He... he just came up and slammed him with that brick. Blindsided him in broad daylight! Who does that?"

Victor kneels next to the man and checks his breathing. "He's still alive. Barely."

"Doctor's coming," says the teen girl. Victor nods.

"Who did it?" he asks.

"Goddamn Klaus, that's who," someone shouts. "He's a no-good ratbag, that one. Everyone knows it."

"Who?"

"Klaus! I don't know his last name. Does odd jobs around here. He's also a bully and thief. We've got him this time though. Chased him. He's hunkered down in that low entrance to the basement. Right over there."

Victor looks to where the people are pointing. A group with rocks and sticks are gathered at the top of a set of stairs, shouting down into the stairwell.

"My God..."

"Go grab him!"

Stunned, Victor rises and walks to the stairs. In his limited days as a policeman, he's had little to do other than deal with drunks and rambunctious kids. Now here he is, looking to actually arrest a violent criminal and he doesn't have a partner with him. He takes a gulp and pushes to the front of the crowd. There's a stone stairwell below sidewalk level. At the bottom of the steps is a tall, heavyset blond man. People above have thrown rocks at him and he's bleeding from his forehead. An iron gate blocks the entrance to the building, effectively trapping him in the stairwell. Klaus is hanging on the gate, rocking his weight back and forth. He's managed to tear one of the hinges loose. If he manages to pull the bars free, that entrance could become an escape route.

"Stop right there!" Victor commands. But Klaus keeps rocking.

"Where does this guy live?" Victor asks.

"Not anywhere, really. Empty buildings. Barely speaks English. Mostly some kind of German that even the other Germans around here don't recognize."

"North country," says a man with a German accent. "Low German."

Victor doesn't care. He needs to arrest this man for assault. He reaches for his gun, changes his mind, and pulls out his billy club.

"Okay, Klaus, let's go." He shouts as he taps the hickory baton on a railing.

But just then, the criminal's rocking efforts pay off. He dislodges the gate. Flinging it aside, he kicks in the door and disappears into the building's basement. Victor bounds down the stairs and follows. He can hear footsteps running through a hall. But in the dim light, he doesn't see much. As he moves forward, he can make out the sloping back of a staircase. Klaus reaches the bottom of the stairs, grabs the banister, spins, and runs upward. Victor follows. It's an open stairway with a railing and spindles.

Victor reaches through the spindles and catches Klaus by the ankle. The tall man crashes down hard.

"I said stop, goddamn it!"

The German shouts something Victor doesn't understand, then manages to kick free and crawls upward.

Victor knows the man won't run toward the front of the building. That's where the crowd is. He follows Klaus up, figuring his quarry will make a turn at the top and run toward the rear.

Klaus reaches the top of the stairs. As Victor suspected, the big man runs toward the back of the hallway. A large window at the end is blocked open with a long piece of wood. Klaus half-dives and half-slides through that window on his belly. He lands three feet below, on the roof of a porch. Victor dives through too, managing to accelerate on the leap – enough so he can tackle Klaus as the man tries to stand. The two of them tumble and roll toward the edge of the porch. When they reach the edge, they drop away.

It's seven feet to the ground. Victor spins as they plunge and he manages to hold Klaus beneath him as they hit the dirt. By landing on top, he manages to drive his shoulder into Klaus' chest. The man's body softens the landing for Victor. He hears a gasping exhale and knows that he's knocked the wind out of the criminal.

Handcuffs out, Victor quickly twists the German's arm and subdues him while he struggles to inhale. Victor lets him catch his breath, then pulls Klaus to his feet. He hears a moan and a wince, and he wonders if maybe he broke the man's ribs.

When Victor walks his captive back to the front of the building, the crowd cheers. Other officers have arrived. They stop the crowd from seeking revenge and they help transport the offender back to the station. Victor is congratulated and thanked.

Back home that night, Victor feels a sense of pride, but also a strange emptiness. For the first time, he feels like a real police officer. He managed to run down a violent criminal, taking him off the streets. But he also remembers the look of the man. There was a confused sense of defeat in Klaus' face. Victor can guess his story. He was poor. He likely left Germany to come to Boston looking for new opportunities. But he can't speak the language enough to get himself hired. He doesn't even speak the same dialect of Boston's other Germans. So where does that leave him?

*Isolated.* Then desperate, Victor thinks. But the man's mistake was to try to steal and strong-arm his way out of his situation.

And that's where Victor came in.

*Well, I guess this is just what cops do.*
And then he falls asleep.

# Chapter 27

## *Fox Hunt*

It's nearly dusk as Devlin traverses the street where, a few days before, he found the litter of puppies. He's been stopping there occasionally to look over the fence. So far, everything has been fine. The mother is always there, looking attentive. Last time he checked, the puppies were larger and their eyes were opening.

The light is low as he approaches, and he sees a strange sight. A fuzzy dark-red shadow wriggles out from under the fence. He hears squeaking and yelping. It takes a moment, but Devlin realizes a crafty fox has dug its way into the yard. It's grabbed one of the puppies and it's making its escape.

Devlin stops dead. His blood boils. It may not be the same puppy he rescued, but that doesn't matter. He's not someone who usually feels protective, but in this moment, he decides this isn't the way it's going to end for the little dog.

The fox hasn't seen him yet. Devlin slips into the shadow of a tree and inches forward as the animal looks left and right. Then it starts to trot toward him. Devlin can hear low squeals from the puppy in its mouth. But just before the fox reaches the tree, the animal's senses tingle. He stops, sniffs, then starts to back away.

Devlin jumps out and gives chase. The fox can easily outmaneuver him, but it makes a bad mistake. It tries to push between a tree and the fence where it can't quite fit. It tries to back out, but Devlin is spry enough to grab it by the scruff of the neck. Lifting the fox high, he uses his other hand to pry the puppy loose from its jaws. When the pup drops, the fox howls and bites at Devlin. But the action is quickly ended when the old southerner swings the beast hard against the slats of the fence. Once, twice. He bashes in the animal's skull and drops it, lifeless, onto the walk.

The puppy is injured. He bleeds from a pair of puncture wounds on its back. Devlin runs his hands along the animal's legs, then sides. Nothing seems broken. There's no blood coming from his nose or mouth. Hopefully the wounds are minor, with no deeper internal injuries.

Carriages go by. No one gives him a second glance. Devlin strokes the pup, retraces his steps, and returns the dog to his mother, again using his method of reaching over the fence and dropping it right onto the mother's chest.

Then he slides his hands into his coat pocket and heads home, gaze focused on the road in front of him.

# Chapter 28

## *Reclamation*

As her train approaches the outskirts of Boston, Amanda reminds herself she has just a small bit of money in her pocket, and no place to call home. There's no apartment to return to. No chest of drawers full of neatly pressed clothes. No oval prints of relatives hanging in gilded frames. She still feels like a nomad – with both the limits and freedoms that come with a nomadic life.

Her wandering life must come to an end. But she's not at all sure how she will reestablish herself. And there are so many changes in her life. So much to absorb and understand.

Victor Marius? Surprisingly alive.

Jeb Thomas? Out of her life.

The Morgans? Hopefully, awaiting her visit.

And the train chugs home.

The first thing she does after exiting the station is to find a rooming house. She checks with three places in the immediate neighborhood and finally finds an inexpensive house with an available bed in a shared room. She pays three dollars and fifty cents for seven days. She then finds the streetcar that will carry her to the Morgans' neighborhood. She walks the final two blocks toward their brownstone. Along the way, she tries to gather her thoughts and decide what to say.

Across the street, a boy of about thirteen tosses a cigarette on the ground, grinding the butt out near a pile of other butts. Movement catches his eyes. This is why he's been standing here. He has been watching, and this must be the woman he's been paid to look for.

Slipping around the corner, he runs in the direction of the docks.

Amanda's knock on the front door of the Morgan's lovely and imposing home is answered by Beverly, who regards her coolly at first, then nods a formal greeting.

"I received your telegraph," Beverly acknowledges. "Jasper and Jonathan fixed the wheel on your steam car, and they made sure the boiler will work. I take it you're here to remove it?"

"Yes. Thank you. How much do I owe you for the storage?"

"Nonsense," Beverly says. "We know your circumstances. No payment needed. I'm just glad to have it out of here."

Upstairs, Amanda hears a thumping sound, and the opening of a door. "Beverly?" a man's voice calls out. "Are you down there? Who's here?"

"Just a minute, dear!"

Amanda recognizes Jonathan's voice. She'd love to see him. It would be nice to chat with him. Enjoy his attention. And for that very reason, Beverly is not about to call up to him, nor tell him who is here. Amanda resigns herself to leaving as quickly as possible.

She also realizes she will have to walk halfway around the block, rather than through the house, to get to their carriage barn.

"I could use his help, you know. To roll it out. To get it started."

Beverly sighs. "All right. I'll let him know that you are here. Jasper too. They'll be along in a bit, I'm quite sure."

Amanda thanks her and wanders down the block then through an alley until she reaches the carriage house. She unbolts the big door and slides it sideways, then brushes some spider webs out of the way.

There's still some coal in the bed of the wagon, and a small pile on the floor, probably hauled there by Jonathan. She collects the coal plus some bits of wood and paper and starts tossing them into the fire box. But she won't light the fire yet. Remembering how the choking smoke built up in the building the first time she drove the wagon inside, she decides to wait until they can push it out.

"Well, hello, my dear," Jonathan calls as he walks across the backyard. "Good to see you're safe and sound." As usual, he wears a fine brown suit and a black tie.

She runs to give him a hug. He gives her a fatherly peck on the cheek.

"Jasper's going to join us. Did you see the adjustments we made?" He shows her the reinforced hubs and the new bands of iron they've attached to the perimeter of the wheels. "Just like a sturdy wagon now, see? This should give these wheels the strength to keep them turning for quite a while."

Five minutes later, Jasper comes around the corner and shouts hello. As Amanda walks toward him, he smiles an impossibly big smile and shows her something he's been hiding behind his back.

Her eyes grow large, and her hands cover her mouth. In his extended hands, Jasper holds her puzzle box. Or maybe she should call it Victor's puzzle box now. It's assembled and polished to perfection.

She squeals, grabs it, holds it high, and spins around, like a ballerina with a bouquet of flowers.

"You found it! How? Where?"

"Oh, I didn't find it. Jonathan did. Do you want to tell her the tale, my friend?"

With great effort, they push the heavy car out into the yard and light the boiler fire as Jonathan shares the story.

"Oh, I went to the police station a couple times. But they never had it. At least that's what they claimed. The fact is, they found it inside a safe right after they took the safe from that Chinaman's shop."

"Chen Lu," Jasper adds.

"Exactly."

"So, he *did* have something to do with the disappearance! I always thought so," Amanda says with disdain.

"Yes, he did. Or at least he was holding it for someone. But when the police managed to get the safe open, and they emptied it, they just put the contents in a bag and set it aside. No one ever made note of what was in the bag. It didn't get logged, so the police had no real record of it. It just sat on a shelf. If someone hadn't tried to steal it from the police station, it might never have been rediscovered."

"Who tried to steal it?"

"Some police officer actually. It was quite the comedy of errors, I hear. But once he was caught, they officially had the box and added it to their inventory. That's when we finally found it."

Amanda starts to take the box apart, remembering most of the major moves. Jasper steps forward when she gets stymied.

"This level is a new one," he says. "We just discovered it a few days ago." He pops open the big compartment and shows her what's inside.

"And… I have no idea what this piece is," he says as he pulls out the mysterious metal coil. "It appears to be something electronic. It must have been important for him to hide it so deep in the box."

Amanda takes the part and holds it up to the light. A few days ago, she would have had no clue about it. But after viewing the sketches in Victor's diary, plus Nikola Tesla's recent drawings, she recognizes it for exactly what it is.

"It's a coil used as part of an electric circuit," she says matter-of-factly. "A coil that's capable of creating a spark that causes a radio wave."

Jasper looks impressed. "I don't know much about that. So, you really think that's what it is?"

"I know it is. Someone explained it to me. And I also know something else." She smiles at the men, like her next bit of news is the best of all. "It turns out the owner of this box isn't dead after all. Can you believe that? He's very much alive and living somewhere in this city."

"Marvelous!" Jonathan exclaims. "Do you want to return the box to him? Maybe meet him?"

"Maybe someday," she says. "But at the moment, I have no idea how to reach him."

They shovel more coal and wood onto the fire. Once the wagon's tank starts to boil, it quickly builds a full head of steam, Amanda climbs in. She tucks the box under the seat and pulls the lever to engage the gears.

"Thank you. Both of you," she shouts over the roar. "I really mean that. You've done so much for me by fixing this old wagon, and by finding this box. I don't know what I'd have done without you."

She leans down to kiss their foreheads then drives out of the yard.

When she reaches the street, the hissing wagon once again draws stares. But this time, she doesn't care. In fact, the attention is kind of fun.

Her plan is simple. She will drive back toward her new rooming house and park the wagon somewhere nearby. She will try to find a buyer for it. That should be simple enough. She will attract enough attention that surely someone will be interested. If nothing else, someone may want to take it apart, to use the boiler and steam engine to power another piece of equipment, maybe factory machines if it stays in the city. Or if it ends up on a farm, maybe a belt or a hoist to lift things up into a barn loft.

But as she drives, a wonderful thought occurs to her. She looks down at the box. She thinks of its contents, especially the coil that Jasper discovered.

Then she has a new thought, and she smiles.

# Chapter 29

## *Pretensions*

Amanda powers the steam wagon through the back streets of Boston, stopping at a handful of businesses along the way. One is a blacksmith shop. Another is a maker of industrial boilers. Still another, a repairer of trolley cars. At each place, she asks if anyone is interested in purchasing the steam engine. She even offers to give a percentage of the sale to anyone who can bring her a buyer.

The boiler shop seems interested, and the owner allows her to park the wagon on his property.

"Can't say as I'll be able to get much for it," he says. "But I'm willing to give it a try."

Back at her rooming house, Amanda spends much of the evening poring over the puzzle box, examining it, and looking for clues as to how its final level can be opened. The last part, the bottom level, is the teak extension Victor added himself. But she's not able to make any headway there. Eventually she falls asleep, surrounded by pieces of the box.

The next morning, as she sits eating toast and jam with the other residents of the house, she hears a knock on the front door. The owner of the home answers it and finds a lad of about thirteen standing on the porch.

"Does a woman named Amanda live here?" he inquires.

Amanda comes to the door and eyes him coolly.

"You don't have to answer. I know who you are," he says. "I'm supposed to deliver a message. I'm supposed to tell you that Jeb would like to see you. In fact, he's waiting around the corner." He points down the street. "That's all he wanted me to say. Just come out to see him if you'd like."

He turns to leave, but Amanda stops him. "Wait? How did you find me?" she demands. "How did Jeb know I was here?"

The lad smiles. He's not supposed to say anymore, but he's obviously proud of his amateur detective work. So, he brags. "When you went to see that old man and old lady. I got paid to keep an eye out for you. I told Jeb. Then I came back to follow you. Simple, eh?"

Amanda shakes her head, looking down the street. "Just around that corner, you say?"

The youngster nods.

"Thank you. Yes, I'll see him. Tell him to wait there. I'll be along in about ten minutes. I need to freshen up."

After shutting the door, Amanda runs to her room, gathers her things, and heads out the back door. She holds a pillowcase containing all her belongings, including the box. But she stops for a moment near the base of the porch. A moment later, she pushes a loose board aside in the back fence, and slips out. She hurries up a path that leads away from the rooming house. One hundred feet down that path, a man steps out and smiles at her. It's Jeb. The invitation from the boy had been little more than a ruse. Jeb must have known she would run, and he figured out her direction.

"Hello, Amanda," he says soothingly. "Good to see you again."

She hugs the pillowcase to her chest. "What are you doing here, Jeb? I don't want to see you." At this point, the only way to avoid him is to retreat back the way she came. She starts to back up. Fast as she is, she is not certain she can outrun him, especially with her dress on.

Jeb holds up his hands in surrender. "You don't need to be afraid of me! I didn't come here to do anything but talk."

"Well, I don't want to talk with you. I think we've said quite enough."

"Amanda," he pleads, "you left without saying good-bye. All that we had together… and you just up and left."

She shakes her head. "We had more together than I realized, Jeb. We had problems together. We had lies between us. And when I found that you sometimes beat people up as part of your job, well, that was a big problem for me. The fact that you were far less than honest with me on several occasions – that just made things worse."

He nods. "I know. And that's why I wanted to leave that job. I'm done with that. You understand that, right? That's not where I want to be anymore. I didn't stay in Montana. I didn't go to San Francisco. I want to be with you."

He smiles at her with that devilish, handsome, earnest grin that first melted her heart so many weeks ago. She feels that same tug again and tries to resist.

"Yes. I still do want to be with you," he continues. "Can't you see that?"

Amanda looks at the sky.

"I've crossed more than a thousand miles just to catch up with you. I gave up on my work, just to find you again. Why do you think I would do that?"

She closes her eyes. "I don't know, Jeb. Why don't you just tell me?"

He eyes her pillowcase. "Because I care for you. Because I thought we were going to build a life together." He swallows hard, and adds, "Because I love you."

Amanda shivers at the words. Back in Montana, she had been close to telling him the same thing. Very close. Now she doesn't want to hear it.

"One of us was kidding ourselves back there, Jeb. Either it was you, convincing yourself I would be the perfect woman, keeping house while you continued with your misdeeds. Or it was me, kidding myself that you could ever be more than, well, whatever you are."

"What I am is changed. I just told you that." He steps forward. "And I really do love you."

She doesn't back away, but she does turn her head to avoid him as he reaches to stroke her hair.

"Don't," she whispers. "You're not the man I want. Not now. And I'm not at all what you think I am. I'm not even what I thought I was. We're done, Jeb."

He sees her hug the pillowcase even more tightly. And as he sees her turn to go, he notices there are several items inside, including the outline of a square box-like object. He fears the contents of that case may be slipping away. Instinctively, he reaches to grab it.

"What are you doing?" she cries as his hand grasps the fabric. "Jeb? Let go!"

"Amanda? Please. Wait! I... I love you..."

As she retreats, he continues to pull at the case, eventually wrenching it free from her arms.

"Jeb? Jeb!"

But his focus has obviously shifted. If she's not coming back to him, he will at least have the box. "That's right! If you leave me, then at least I get this much from you!"

He yanks open the pillowcase and thrusts his hand inside. He feels some clothes, an apple, a notebook, and little else. Angry, he dumps the sack's meager contents on the ground. He kicks at it. Still nothing. She's not carrying the puzzle box. The square he thought he saw was just the outline of the notebook.

"Where is it?" he growls.

"Where is what?" She backs up as she speaks. "Jeb. You're scaring me."

"You know very well what I'm—"

But she's already gone. She runs back down the alley, through the fence, and into the back door of the house. Jeb pursues, following her into the kitchen and through to the dining area.

The other women scream. Jeb grabs Amanda, swinging her around. "Where is it? Where *is* it?!" Amanda flails and kicks at him.

"Which room is hers?" He yells to the other women. "Just tell me which room she's staying in, then I'll be gone."

They all look at him with fearful eyes.

"Now!"

One of the women points to a small room tucked off the side of the dining room.

Jeb lets go, and Amanda dashes out the front door. He enters the shared bedroom and practically turns it inside out, pulling out drawers. Pulling back bedclothes, flipping mattresses, and looking in and under everything. Then he retreats. He found nothing, and now he's completely lost Amanda too. He curses at the cowering housemates and trots out the front door. Amanda is long gone.

*How did it come to this? I've never acted like this before!* Jeb mutters to himself. He continues to run, down the street and away from the house. He focuses all his anger on quickening his pace.

By not staying in Montana, and by giving up on his plan to travel to San Francisco, Jeb has closed some very important doors in his life. Yet he has gained nothing in return. Damn woman. Couldn't she see that? Couldn't she see how much he had to offer?

And where the hell did she hide that box?

# Chapter 30

## *Wire Crew*

Victor Marius has a few days off from his police duties, and he's back at work for the electric company. His wire crew is very glad to see him. Finally, they have some substantial work hours assigned and they can earn some pay.

"They was talking about shutting us down, Vic. You know, until they could hire a new supervisor," one of the men said. "Glad you're back. You had us right worried!"

"I know. I'm sorry," Victor says earnestly. "First, they let us go, then they hire us back. It happens at their whim. Now, I'm working two jobs, and keeping up as best I can."

"I hear that," says another one of the crew. "I've been swinging a hammer myself when we're not working here."

Victor looks at all the equipment piled beside their horse-drawn wagons. "Looks like we have a lot of work to do. What do you say we get moving?"

They quickly load their carts with spools of rubber-clad copper wire. They also take splicing equipment, hooks, and boxes of heavy glass and ceramic insulators. They intend to follow behind a pole crew that's been drilling earth and setting wooden poles. That crew is making its way north near the coastal towns.

Victor's team will add the wires to the poles, stringing along the highway as far as they can reach before they run out of supplies. If new supplies can reach them every day, they should be able to reach thirty-five miles or more over the next several weeks. Victor plans to work when he can, and he will give his team explicit instructions for what they need to do while he is away – especially when he is back at his police job for two to three days each week.

In the area just north of Boston, at least eight highly competitive power companies have sprouted up. Some generate power from small dams. Other entrepreneurs have built coal-fired boilers that spin large generators. No matter how the electricity is generated, each of these companies has the same need – wire crews to help them build networks to distribute their product. The company Victor works for has a simple plan. Besides selling their own electricity, they also rent out their wire crews to the other electric providers. This not only gives them an additional source of revenue, but also provides first-hand insight into their competitors' systems. Victor knows his company's long-term plan is to buy or merge with other companies, so this kind of insider knowledge, about who is building quality systems and doing a good job with the wiring, is highly valuable.

"Is it true we're getting extra pay for our work?" someone asks Victor.

"Well, they've offered bonuses if we reach our quota of miles," Victor explains. "Yes, I think we can do it. And if things work out, we could have steady work until mid-fall."

One of his men looks down the road. "You know, as we get farther from the city, it's going to take more and more time for you to make the trip back to Boston whenever you work your police shifts."

"True," says Victor.

"At some point, you're going to have to make a decision, right? Stick with us? Or go be a copper full time?"

Victor chuckles. "Yeah, I know that decision is looming. But for now? I don't have to worry."

With the crew constantly on the road, the power company has provided them with four tents and a food wagon. Victor's actually glad for the chance to get out of his lab. He's also glad to take a break from walking his police beat.

Then there is his ulterior motive for wanting to be on the road.

In two days, Professor Alton will start broadcasting a radio signal using the brand-new spark-gap generator they've designed.

When Victor is working the wires, wherever he is, he plans to set up a portable antenna and use a rechargeable battery to run a receiver the pair have built together. Truth be told, his receiver and antenna have been built using parts he's borrowed from the power company. That's one thing that made him decide to continue working the wires. Access to free parts.

As far as Victor can see, heading out on the road is a perfect solution. He will be able to continue his tests, and at the same time, he'll get paid – all while spending some time in the sun.

# Chapter 31

## *The Complaint*

The police officer takes notes and asks for a description.

"So, you say he came right into the house? Grabbing at one of your housemates, and then pawing through her room?"

The girl nods. She's Irish. Right off the boat. She points to the back door, and then to Amanda's room. "Sure an' he did. Chasing her, he was! Ran right through here, and he grabbed her. But then let her go, that one. He stormed into her room. He seemed to be looking for something. Threw things all over the room, yelling like a banshee!"

The woman answering his questions, Nieve O'Reilly, lives in Amanda's rooming house and works in a laundry down the street.

"Who is the owner of this house?" the officer demands.

"Mrs. McCaughey," Nieve replies. "But she was upstairs at the time. She didn't see anything. Not until it was all over."

The officer nods. "And what of the woman who was chased? Why are you filing the complaint instead of her?"

"Well, you know, I haven't seen her since she ran away. I thought it best to contact you in case he caught up to her and did her some harm. I pray to God he hasn't. And I'm also worried he may come back here."

The officer nods. "Do you have the woman's name? We'll keep an eye out for her."

"Yes," she says. "When she first moved in, she introduced herself as Amanda. Amanda Grant, I believe. She's only been living here for a day or so."

"So not long at all?"

"That's the trouble with the rooming houses, don't you know? You never know what you're getting yourself into when you're living with strangers." Nieve smiles at the cop and pulls a strand of reddish-blonde hair out of her face, tucking it behind her ear.

The police officer nods and tells her that he'll check back in a day or so. In the meantime, they'll keep an eye out for both the woman and her attacker.

"And if you see her," he adds, "please contact us again. I'm a little curious why she's kept this matter to herself."

As the policeman leaves, he makes plans to swing by his station house. One of the rules they have is that, for every complaint filed, they have to check the names against a set of small white cards kept on file at the front desk. Those cards list the names of anyone who has an outstanding warrant for their arrest.

# Chapter 32

## *Alternative*

Devlin Richards presses his fingertips together and rests them against his forehead. Eyes closed, he tries to listen and fully absorb what Jeb is telling him.

"… and that's why I think it's the only way we're going to find her." Jeb finishes his explanation with a little shrug.

There's a long pause before Devlin speaks.

"Let me get this straight. You tried to approach her already, but you totally muffed the effort. You pushed your way into her rooming house. You didn't get the box, and now she's run away again?"

Jeb nods.

"And you went alone for what reason exactly?" He looks Jeb up and down, then he rises and paces the small room. "You and I had a deal," he continues. "You were going to provide the information, and I was going to do the grab. Correct?"

Jeb says nothing.

"You're goddamn right that's correct. I'm supposed to be part of it. Plus, you said you wanted to keep your nose clean. We were supposed to split the proceeds." He looks back at Jeb. "Wasn't that the original plan? Starting many months ago, before you went west? Wasn't that still the plan once you came back?"

"Listen," Jeb protests. "I wasn't cutting you out. I was simply trying to contact her. You may remember that she and I were together for many weeks. I still want to get back with her, and I was trying to find her. I was lucky, with help from our young spy. And thanks to him, we found her right off. You weren't around, so I had to move on it while I had an opportunity."

"Yeah. Great job. You scared her away."

"I did," Jeb admits.

"I don't think you're cut out for this kind of work, union man. What's worse, I don't believe I can trust you. If you had found that box, you wouldn't be here right now, would you?"

"Yes, I would. Think what you want. But I looked and I didn't find it. Of course, she isn't going to have anything to do with me anymore, and she and the box are still out there. We obviously need to keep working together, and we need to be a little more creative in our endeavors."

Devlin is silent for a while. "What I really want to do," he says, "is tell you to go to hell and then to bust your head. But I want that box, and I don't know any other way to get it but to work with you."

Jeb nods, relieved.

"What we need," Devlin sniffs, "is to corner her."

"Yes," Jeb agrees. "I know we do. She's wily, that one. She slips away too easily when we aren't prepared. First, we must make sure she actually has the box, then we need to close in fast."

"And how do you suggest we do that?"

Jeb grins. "I've still got our boy watching the rooming house. Same one that kept an eye on the Morgans'. He swears Morgan and that Jasper guy turned the box over to her. My guess is, she's not going to stay at that rooming house anymore. But the box must be hidden somewhere near there and she'll have to go back for it. We'll stake things out and we then we'll make our move."

Devlin remains silent. Fingers stroking his scar, he just looks out the window, and he quietly makes a plan of his own.

# Chapter 33

## *Boston Calling*

When Jeb's intrusion made her flee from the rooming house, Amanda ran for nearly a mile, zigzagging through the streets until she was sure Jeb wasn't following her. Then she slipped into an apothecary and sat at a lunch counter, with her back to the door. She ordered quinine water with lime and stole quick glances through the window for over an hour. She needed time to digest what just happened.

Jeb had just appeared out of nowhere, looking to reconcile. But, obviously, he also came looking for the box. Why might he want it?

What she does know is that she needs to escape once again. But it must be done correctly this time. She can leave no trail.

Eventually her eyes drift to a corner of the apothecary's main room. There, bolted to a wall, is a big wooden telephone. There's a hand-held earpiece and a crank on the side.

She's never used a telephone before. But her thoughts immediately turn to Nikola Tesla. He said he had a phone. He provided his local number and details for the long-distance operator. If she could talk to him, maybe, just maybe, he could help her.

"Excuse me," she says to the man behind the counter. "That telephone. Is that for anyone to use?"

The druggist nods. "Yes, it is. We rent it, 5 cents a minute. Plus another quarter if you call outside of Boston."

"My goodness, that's expensive. How do I pay?"

"Well, usually I just help you place the call and keep track of your time. Then you can pay me when you're done."

She smiles. "I think I'd like to try it. Can you help me connect to an operator who can place a call through to New York?"

The druggist lifts the receiver, talks to an operator, and helps make the connection. He hands her the earpiece, and she awkwardly places it against her ear. She leans forward to be near the black mouthpiece mounted on the phone's oak face. She feels nervous. She can hear the Boston operator talking to the main New York exchange, and then the

New York operator rings a neighborhood switchboard where someone, in turn, calls the number at Tesla's home.

"Hello?" he says in his Croatian accent.

"Call for Mr. Tesla from Boston. Go ahead please, ma'am."

Amanda takes a deep breath. "Mr. Tesla? Hello. This is Amanda Grant. I met you a couple days ago." It seems strange for her to hear the sound of her own voice echoing through the line. Thank goodness she doesn't usually need to make telephone calls.

"Who?" Tesla responds. "Wait. Oh, yes... yes. I remember. Hello, Miss Grant."

"I made it back to Boston," she continues, "and now I have a question for you. Did you ever hear from Victor again?"

"Yes. Indeed, I did!"

"You did? And how do I find him?" Her face immediately reflects disappointment when she hears he's gone out of the city to work with his wire crews.

"I see. And he won't return for weeks, you say? ....."

"Oh," Tesla responds, "I think he will return on occasion. He still does part-time work for the police."

She listens to Tesla's voice, static-filled and impossibly distant. He adds, "But to me, the exciting part is that he's continuing his radio work. Even as he's on the road. He will be running all sorts of tests. He's going to try receiving radio messages from several different places. Isn't that exciting?"

"I see," Amanda replies. "Sir, can I ask you for a favor? Do you remember some of those sketches you made for me?"

"Yes, of course, I remember."

"Well, I found something of Victor's. ... Yes, it's a coil, just like the one you drew for me."

On the wall next to the phone hangs a clipboard and a pencil. It's meant for people to write messages as they talk on the phone. Amanda starts to draw a diagram as she talks.

"Yes, I know it's complicated. But I have a rough idea how it works, from Victor's writings. Yes, sir. I have more questions... can we start by talking about the wires and how they connect?"

She listens for a long time. She asks some very detailed questions about the circuit design and how to activate it. She also corrects Tesla once, saying that Victor's diary entry listed a slightly different way to power up the coil.

"And what about the power source itself?"

She writes down details about amps and voltage. When all her design questions are answered, she asks one final question. Her face holds a look of disappointment again when she hangs up the phone. "I don't know if I can do this," she mutters to herself.

"You were on there for a long time," the druggist says. "Over twenty minutes."

She nods, pays him, then heads for the street.

# Chapter 34

## *Cornered*

Devlin's searching, and his patience, finally pays off.

Not far from where he first spotted Irene, he sees her again. This time, no passing trains block his way. He's able to follow her at a distance. In his mind, he sorts through all the ways she wronged him. Stealing his savings. Disappearing without even saying goodbye. He very much wants to settle the score with her. But he must proceed carefully.

He watches as she shops for food, buys a newspaper, then walks up a side street toward a small house. She heads around to the rear and he follows, staying hidden by a group of bushes. Irene climbs a set of exterior stairs and enters a second-story apartment. Devlin figures that must be where she's living now.

He waits a few minutes, then stealthily climbs the treads. He presses his back against the siding so he can't be viewed from inside.

He listens for a few minutes. There are no other voices, so he suspects she's alone.

He waits until a noisy wagon rumbles through the neighborhood, and uses that as cover to kick the door in. Irene's surprise is total. She is sitting at a table, reading her paper and eating a bowl of peaches with sweet cream. Her mouth falls open and her spoon stops halfway to her mouth.

"Hello, Irene," Devlin says with a sneer. "Nice to see you again. We need to talk."

# Chapter 35

## *Breakthrough*

It sounds a bit like fingers snapping. Or maybe like someone tapping a rolled newspaper against a table. But the small static-like crackle at the end of each tap reveals its source.

Victor Marius has been packing for his trip and running some experiments in his lab. He smiles as he watches a spark spit out from his new coil – over and over again. It's the best example he's produced so far, and the spark generates a nice solid radio signal each time it occurs. This version of his spark gap generator is oval and has a sleeker and safer design than the disk style he was using before.

In retrospect, he's sorry he tossed that first disk into his puzzle box. But it was the best disk design he had at that time, and he thought it was worth saving.

To extend the test, Victor drags a receiver farther and farther from the source of the spark. First across the room, then out to the empty gravel lot next to his building, and then down the road. Satisfied that the signal remains strong even as he moves away from the source, he powers down the machines and waits for Professor Alton to arrive.

Twenty minutes later, the old man rides in on a borrowed horse, at nearly full gallop.

"I heard it! I heard it, Victor! Three miles away, and it came through loud and clear on my receiver. Sounded just like we were in the same room."

Victor nods. "Good, good. But we've been here before. This time we want things to be different. Stronger."

Professor Alton interrupts him. "It is! I measured the signal at nine point three. That's what I saw on my gauge. What did you have?"

Victor smiles, raising his hands. "Yes. The same! Nine point three!"

They laugh and shake hands.

"Yes! We've never been above a three before, Victor! You know what this means? No loss. Three miles and absolutely zero signal loss. My god, that's a huge milestone!"

"How far do you think we can go?" Victor asks. "Can we actually get up to 100 miles like we were trying to reach back in June? Back when I was listening from the ship?"

"Think? I know we can! Of course, we can. And I'll bet we can do it with less than 30 percent loss across that distance. And that would mean we might be able to reach even farther."

Victor beams. "I knew it. We've finally cracked it, my friend. This will be huge."

The professor paces the room. He rubs his chin. "Yes. But so much to be done though. How much of your design is actually written down?"

"All of it!" Victor replies. 'Well, most of it. I think."

Professor Alton waves the comment away. "Come inside. Show me the spark generator. Show me the drawings. We'll finish them. Polish them. You sign them and I'll go to a patent attorney with the drawings in the morning. We're going to get this on record quickly for you, Victor."

# Chapter 36

## *Vengeance*

Irene tries to stand but Devlin forces her back into her chair. He circles the table, glaring, waiting for her to speak. At last, she does so.

"What happened to your face?"

"The cost of doing business is what happened."

He continues walking around her, pulling his knife when he's behind her. When he comes back in front, he grabs her by the chin and holds the blade in front of her eyes. She looks at it in fear.

"Now let's talk about our business. And I don't think you want to end up with a scar like mine."

She closes her eyes.

"You betrayed me, dear," Devlin continues. "Quite deeply."

She starts to shake. "I know, Devlin. I'm so sorry."

"Are you?"

"I am, Devlin, whether you accept that or not. It was just the circumstances."

He goes back to pacing. Visibly furious. "Circumstances? We were becoming a team! At least I thought we were." He snorts, then leans over the table. "Let's start with the money you took. Where is it?"

"It's gone. Spent. It helped me survive."

"There's no way you could have spent it all."

"I had debts too. And people to appease. Money can go very quickly, Devlin. You know that."

He looks her in the eyes for several moments, then slaps her hard with a backhand across her cheek. Her head spins with the impact, but she doesn't fall. She holds her cheek. Tears well up a bit, but she doesn't cry.

"Let's see if you can address that question again."

"I have nothing to give you."

Devlin moves through the apartment. He opens cabinets and drawers. He looks everywhere. After several minutes of searching, he only finds two dollars and a few coins.

"This? This is what you have? This is how you live? After taking so much from me?"

"I don't know what to say, Devlin."

He pulls a chair up directly across from her and keeps the knife in view as he looks into her eyes. "I don't understand how you could just leave me. No breaking it off. No goodbye. Nothing. And on top of that, you stole from me. You stole most of what I had. It hurt. And I just want to know why." He looks deep into her eyes. "So, tell me."

She looks away. "I don't know, Devlin. You and I are businesspeople. We partner when we need to. We break things off when we need to."

Devlin bites his lip. "You meant far more to me than just a business partner, Irene."

She nods. "I know."

"But I guess I didn't mean more than that to you, did I?"

She takes a long breath. Then looks away.

Devlin closes his eyes.

"I'm going to ask you one more time about my money. But before I do, I want to know how you could do that. To make me feel like I meant something to you. And I want to hear you say that there really was, indeed, nothing there."

She sighs, and finally looks back at him. "And that's the problem with you, Devlin. You *want* me to say this. You *want* me to feel that. You spend too much time wanting. I mean that. It was the wanting that drove you to come north in the first place. You told me that. Good lord, the war was over more than twenty-five years ago. But you still want things to be the way they were back then. And you want revenge. You want riches and you want control. And what has any of that done for you?"

He gives her a cool but angry look.

"You also want the power back that your family used to have, but they will never have it again."

"I know we will never get any of that back. But my plan has always been to find and bring back whatever I can."

"And now you magically want love." She starts to rise, but he tells her to sit down.

"What I want is everything that you took from me. Once I get that, we can talk about what I should do with you."

123

Irene tries a different tactic. "I know you aren't all evil, Devlin. I've seen some good in you. For example, you are kind to animals. I'm not sure why, when nothing else seems to matter to you. But at least you have that."

He nods. "Animals don't hate. They don't have an agenda other than survival. I can forgive a wolf for killing to eat. But I can't forgive a Yankee who crushes everything in his path, just to enjoy the destruction."

"But aren't you doing the same? Crushing? Taking? Enjoying it? And what about your family? I know they were well-off before the war. What would they think of where you are now?"

He stares at her. "Stop right now. And for the last time, I'm going to ask, Irene. Where's my money?"

She shakes her head.

Devlin rises, walks toward her, and places the knife against her chest. But then he changes his mind and grips her by the throat instead.

"You ruined everything. You know you did."

"You were ruined before we even met."

He's heard enough. He applies pressure. When she gasps and squirms, he places his hand over her face, mostly so he won't have to look into her eyes.

In a few minutes, the deed is done. He quietly closes the door and descends the outdoor staircase, wiping his eyes as he goes.

# Chapter 37

## *Warrant*

Amanda manages to secure a bed in a new rooming house. Just to be safe, she also stops by a used clothing store to buy herself an inexpensive change of clothes—a simple black skirt and a light-yellow blouse. She also purchases a well-worn coat, a shawl, and a bonnet that fits tightly around her face.

Wearing her new outfit, she walks through the back streets until she nears her previous rooming house. She chose the outfit in order to look like an older woman. Hopefully that will make her less noticeable to anyone watching. She circles the block twice, trying to see if anyone is monitoring the doors. She sees a boy, so she waits down the street until he is distracted. As the sky turns to dusk, she sees him looking up at a woodpecker tapping on a tree. That's when she slips around the side and into the back door. Nieve is in the kitchen, preparing to leave.

"Begorrah," Nieve exclaims. "I thought for sure that man must have caught you!"

Amanda laughs. "No, I managed to slip away. How long did he stay here?"

"Five minutes is all. Ransacked your room, indeed he did. Screamed at us like a madman. Then, just as suddenly, he ran out. I'm so glad he didn't catch you, Amanda. Scary one, he was. Beyond the pale, I'd say."

"Yes. I think I'd agree with that. And what did you do after that?"

"We called the police, of course."

Amanda closes her eyes and sighs. "Well, I guess I should have expected that."

"We gave them your name. Wanted to make sure you stay safe."

Amanda swallows hard, but says nothing.

"Well, anyway, Mrs. McCaughey has some stew on the stove. I'm sure you're welcome to help yourself. I have to go to work now, else I'd stay and chat with you, dear." She pats Amanda's hand. "I dare say, if that kind of intrusion had happened to me, I'd be in much more of a tizzy than you seem to be."

"I'm fine actually," Amanda assures her. She doesn't know how to explain it, but after all the dangers and threats she's endured, this intrusive mission of Jeb's – to reclaim the puzzle box – seems like little more than a minor inconvenience.

"Why are you working in the evening?" she asks Nieve as she helps her put on her coat.

"Oh, I have so much work to do down at the laundry. We need to hire a new girl. The clothes are just piling up. You mentioned you might be looking for work? Why don't you come along? I could introduce you to the manager."

Amanda shakes her head. "Thank you for thinking of me. But my plans have changed. I've already moved to another place, and I'm not even sure how much longer I'll be in Boston."

"Sorry to hear that," Nieve replies. "But suit yourself, dear. Sure'n it's a shame to see you go. You seem like a nice woman. Well, except for the whole man-breaking-in-to-attack-you episode." She gives a quick wink.

After Nieve departs, Amanda looks around to see if anyone is watching. Out the window, she can no longer see the boy. Quietly, she slips into the backyard. At the bottom of the porch, she kicks aside a board that's leaning up against the base. It covers a small hole in the lattice. Amanda had noticed the hole when Jeb sparked her hasty exit from the building. As she was running past, she realized it would be the perfect place to stash the puzzle box. She didn't feel safe carrying it away, knowing that Jeb was looking for her. That turned out to be the right choice.

Down the street, Nieve is near the front door of the laundry when she spies a police officer walking his beat. It's the same man who took the report from her after Jeb's intrusion.

"Hello again, officer! Good to see you!"

The cop smiles and tips his hat. "Yes, Nieve, wasn't that your name? No more trouble at your place, I hope?"

"No, no. It's been fairly quiet, thanks be to God. I don't suppose you had any luck catching our intruder?"

"No, ma'am. Unfortunately, I did not. It's like he disappeared into thin air."

Nieve fans her lightly freckled face with a handkerchief. "Well, maybe you can find some more information. Would you like to talk to the woman that he chased?"

The officer immediately looks interested.

"She's at the rooming house right now," Nieve smiles.

"You don't say? Is she now? Well, maybe I'll just pay her a visit and take her statement."

Nieve smiles, believing she's done her good deed for the day. "I'm sure she'd be very glad to see you." She leans closer. "You know, Officer McBride—that is your name, isn't it?"

The man nods.

"Well, sir, you're welcome to stop by to say hello anytime, not just when you're taking a report." She gives him a big smile then opens the door and walks into the hiss and steam of the laundry.

Officer McBride has mixed feelings as he walks toward the rooming house. He kind of likes that woman Nieve. She seems like a good Irish girl. He'd very much like to get to know her better. But on the other hand, he's not sure how she might react if she knew he was planning to arrest her housemate.

After he responded to the initial complaint, he returned to the station to check all the names on the outstanding warrants list. And there was Amanda's name. Wanted for attempted murder, no less!

*Amanda Malcolm*, the report said. Also known by her maiden name, *Amanda Grant*.

McBride pats his gun as he heads up the front steps of the rooming house. Hopefully this woman will come quietly. But either way, she is going to come with him.

The officer walks in the front door, through the empty house, and onto the back porch. He catches Amanda off guard. Despite her protests, they are soon on their way to the station.

# Chapter 38

## *The Thief*

Victor Marius spends four days working on a set of electric lines that stretch north from Boston. Then he rides home for two days to walk his police beat.

It's a rainy Monday when he learns he won't spend this week's shifts on his regular beat. Instead, he's being temporarily reassigned. There's been a problem with pickpockets in another part of the city. It's a neighborhood that sits beside the old orphanage where he used to coach boxing.

"Okay, but what do I do?" Victor asks. "Just stand around watching and hoping I see something?"

His supervisor smiles. "Exactly. We just need to show our face, remember? Make them think we're taking it seriously. You know, that's half of policing. Just making people feel like they're being heard and getting some help."

But within his first couple of hours in the new neighborhood, Victor quickly learns plenty of people are very willing to talk with him. More than just a few wallets have been taken. He soon hears that close to 30 pickpocketing attempts have been made in the past week, and the story is the same for each theft.

The deed is always done by a boy, maybe twelve to fourteen. The descriptions are a little different, so Victor realizes it's not always the same boy. It sounds like there's a group working together.

Their method is to sneak up, bump someone, and then grab something of value during the confusion, often a wallet, a purse, or a watch. The execution sounds fairly amateurish. If they are noticed, the boys stop being sneaky and they just outright grab. They usually are able to outrun whoever is chasing them.

With a few leads written down in his little notebook, Victor stops a couple of boys. They are reluctant to talk at first. But one of their mothers notices what's happening, and she rushes over.

"It's not my boy! Don't you try to pin any of this on my boy!"

"Mom, please," the youngster bellows.

She holds up a finger. "Hush. Let me talk." Then she turns to Victor. "I can tell you who they are, officer."

Victor smiles. "If you can, that would save me a lot of work. What do you know?"

She describes a group of boys who slip away from the orphanage during the day. "There's usually three or four of them. Tallest boy seems to be their leader. I've seen them several times. Up to no good, I'd dare say. They stand over there on that corner, watching and planning. Then they split up. They follow people for a block or so. Wily bunch. Got us all on edge."

A man who's walking past hears what she's saying, and he stops to add some details. Then another woman does the same. In a few minutes, Victor has gathered multiple descriptions, right down to the kind of cap and shoes worn by one of the thieves.

It takes a few hours of walking the neighborhood, but Victor eventually spies one of the lads. The description of his cap helped. But as he closes in, Victor's heart sinks. He knows the boy. It's indeed one of the lads from the orphanage. In fact, it's one of the kids he coached in his old boxing club.

Victor has a sinking feeling as he follows the boy up the street. He watches the youngster scan the crowd. He sees him slow his pace when he spots a possible target. The lad is so busy hunting for something to steal that he doesn't sense Victor as he walks up behind him. As the lad softly and slowly reaches into a woman's open purse, Victor grabs him by the back of his neck.

"Tony! Is that you? Come with me, my boy. We have some things to talk about."

# Chapter 39

## *On Deposit/On Hold*

Jeb's plan is a simple one. He's learned, thanks to his young spy, that Amanda has been hauled off to jail. Maybe that's not a bad thing right now. At least he knows where she is. But he's not sure how long they will be able to keep her there. What he needs to do now is cut off any of her potential escape routes.

Here's what he knows: Her strange steam car has been removed from the Morgans' place. That means she must have moved it, probably somewhere in the vicinity of wherever she's living now. Either that or she sold it or gave it away. She didn't have time to do much else. But if she has it parked someplace, that wagon also might be where the puzzle box is hidden.

He and Devlin patrol the streets of her new neighborhood, up and down, until they finally spot the old steam wagon. When they do, Jeb approaches the owner of the shop, pretending to be a prospective buyer.

"Hey. What's the story with that old Dudgeon?" he asks the boilermaker.

"What, you mean that old steam rig out front? Ain't that something? You ever seen anything like that?"

"No, indeed, I haven't. What's it doing here? You repairing it?"

"No, actually, it's already fixed up. Someone drove it here. Can you believe that? Thing's close to thirty years old and it's still running. The owner wants to sell it."

"That a fact?"

"Yes, indeed."

"Huh. Well, I have a real interest in old engines like that. Have any idea what she wants for it?"

The shop owner rubs his dirty hands on a rag. "Well, it's kind of rare. So, how does sixty-five dollars sound?" He smiles politely, then adds, "And how did you know the owner was a she?"

Jeb stammers but keeps his composure. "Oh, I… um… don't think I did. I meant to say 'how much is she going for?' When I said 'she,' I was really talking about the wagon."

"Ah. Of course," the shop owner says with genuine acceptance. "Well, are you making an offer?"

"Might be… might be. Would you take forty?"

"Not without asking her."

Jeb nods. "Mind if I climb on board and take a closer look?"

"Sure, be my guest."

Jeb goes over the wagon with a fine-toothed comb. He looks in every space capable of holding the box. There's nothing to be found. He's disappointed, but his only hope now is to try to use the wagon as a bargaining chip to meet Amanda again.

He talks again to the shop owner. "Um… I do want to make sure it really works first. So, when I come back, we need to fire it up. Make sure it moves. Is that okay?"

The boilermaker sighs. "That's a lot of work. But if you put down money, I guess that's fair."

Jeb leaves fifteen dollars as a deposit, insisting that the car not be moved, even by the current owner, unless he's notified.

"That should keep Amanda in town for a while," he tells Devlin when they reconnect, "even if she manages to get out of the pokey."

"That's it? That's your whole plan?"

"Not necessarily. That's just insurance. Now we also need to go make friends with someone who works at the jail."

# Chapter 40

## *The Ring*

Elbows on the desk. Head in his hands.

Victor sits in the office of the Boston Police commissioner. His gun and his badge rest in the middle of the big walnut desk. In the hallway behind him, a few staff members look on and whisper.

He doesn't look up when he hears the door close.

The commissioner gives Victor a reassuring pat on the shoulder as he passes. He then slides into his leather desk chair and is silent for several moments. Finally, he speaks.

"Are you all right?"

"I'm as all right as I can be, I guess," Victor says after a long exhale, "given the circumstances."

The commissioner nods. "I have some newspaper men outside. Plus, some mothers' group I've never heard of, and even the head of the orphanage. I won't sugarcoat it, son. They're all angry. I'm not sure what to tell them yet. I wanted to talk to you first."

Victor stares at the green tiles on the floor.

"Maybe you can tell me what happened? Go ahead. Just start at the beginning."

Victor takes a deep breath, then nods.

"I think you already know most of it. That was not my regular beat. I was temporarily assigned there when I came in yesterday. Duty officer told me they were beefing up patrols because kids in the neighborhood were becoming bolder about stealing and pickpocketing."

The commissioner nods. "Kids from the orphanage?"

"Right. That's what I was told. So, first day I went over there, I got some great leads. People seemed plenty fed up with the kids. So that made it easier to get some details."

"Yes, a little community anger always helps."

"So, when I was on the street, I kept my eye out for any of the kids I might know in that neighborhood. Orphanage youth. I used to coach boxing there, you know. So anyway, once I got there, the people I talked to were pretty straightforward about what they were dealing with, with the young pickpockets. Just by asking a few questions, I soon realized that I knew one of the kids involved in the thefts. Not a bad kid really. Just never had any guidance. In fact, when he was..."

The commissioner holds up his hand. "I understand. But for now, just stick to what happened."

"Right... Right. So eventually I managed to find that kid. His name is Tony. I decided to follow him, staying about 50 feet behind. I could see him eyeing purses and looking for men who keep their money clips in their coat pockets, that sort of thing. Now, I didn't call out to Tony. Didn't want to spook him. I just followed. Eventually I saw him closing in on a woman carrying a parasol. She had a bag slung over one shoulder. She stopped at a fruit and vegetable stand. I saw him wait until her hands were full. She was holding the parasol with one hand and a tomato with the other. Then he slipped in close. Slid his hand into her bag and slid out a fat change purse. Did it pretty well too."

The commissioner studies Victor. "I feel like you're avoiding telling me about the shooting."

Victor looks the commissioner in the eye. "No, sir. Not at all. I just want you to know how everything came together. I don't want to leave out any details."

The commissioner nods and gestures for him to continue.

"So, when Tony turned around, I was right there. I grabbed him. Called him by name. I didn't let on what I saw at first. Asked him if he was still strapping on the gloves and taking part in the club. I know he recognized my voice. He looked up and his face dropped when he saw my uniform. He had no idea what to think. He just mumbled 'Oh, hello, coach.'"

"Did he run?"

"No. I thought he might. But he just looked around nervously. I talked to him a bit. He apologized. Gave the change purse back to the lady. Then I pressured him, and he admitted he knew the police were looking for him and the others." He thought they were too smart to get caught."

"Did he have anything else on him? Wallets. Whatever."

"No."

"Really?"

133

"He was carrying nothing. I could tell he was passing. Every time he took something, he likely handed it off to one of the older kids. So, while we were talking, I saw Tony looking around. Looking more nervous. And I saw his gaze go directly toward one of those older kids. That boy was standing up the block. He was wearing a big overcoat even though the day was warm. I figured his coat probably had stolen stuff crammed in every pocket. My guess was that Tony was one of several kids out stealing and passing things off before they could get caught."

"So that other kid. What happened?"

"The other kid saw us looking and quickly turned away. He tried to sidestep and blend in with the crowd."

The commissioner listens to Victor's story, fingers pressed together and resting under his chin.

"So, I followed him. I pulled Tony with me by grabbing his shirt. The older kid turned the corner and went into an alley. I sped up, and when we turned the corner too, I saw the kid's big coat laying there on the ground. Pockets were spilling out all sorts of coins and watches. Guess he decided to dump the evidence. Tried to change his look."

"What happened then?"

"I saw the kid running with something in his hand. I let go of Tony and pushed him into a shop doorway. 'Stay right in there,' I told him. Figured he'll be safe there. And then I chased after the other boy. I don't think that kid realized there was no exit out of that alley. Just buildings. When the kid reached the end, he stopped and looked each way. Stupid place to run to, and he saw that he made a bad mistake. When I got closer, I could finally see what he had in his hand. It was a pistol. A damn pistol. Kid's maybe 13 years old. Where the hell did he get that? So, I drew my pistol too, but I didn't point it at him yet. I kept it tilted at the ground and I hold up my other hand. I tried to calm him. tried to get him to stop. I said I just want to talk with him, you know? I told him I'm not going to shoot him or hurt him or anything as long as he dropped his gun."

The commissioner nods. "And did he?"

Victor bites his lip, then looks toward the hallway. "No, sir. He did not."

"And?"

"We just stood there. Looking at each other. The kid looked around again, like he thought some sort of exit was going to magically appear. I kept pleading with him. 'Drop it. Just drop it,' I said. But instead, he started to raise the gun a little. I just shouted 'no.' He seemed to hesitate, and for a moment I thought that's good. Maybe he's decided to be sensible. Then he started crying. The kid started bawling right there in the street. Said 'I ain't going back to juvie again.' And as the kid cried, Tony came up and stood next to me. My heart dropped right then. I mean, I left Tony in the doorway, right? He was safe there, damn it! But the kid suddenly complicated everything when he caught up to me."

"Why is that?"

Victor bites his lip harder and looks around the room. "Because suddenly, it wasn't just me. Right? It was no longer just me and the other kid facing off and trying to cool things down. No, suddenly Tony was there too, complicating things because he got too close to me. The other kid started to lift his gun. I couldn't let him shoot. If it was just me, maybe I could try to dodge or side-step, or who knows? But now, Tony is next to me in the danger zone, and the kid kept raising his gun. So, I had to make a choice. Should I stop this? I literally had to choose one kid over the other. I don't care if it was a one-second decision. It felt like hours. I didn't want to choose. I just wanted the kid's gun to just… vanish. But it didn't. That forced me. So, I fired quickly. I wanted to aim more. Maybe shoot him in the leg? I don't know. The arm? Maybe even shoot the gun itself, ridiculous as that sounds. But, fuck no. I couldn't do any of that. He was moving fast, so I reacted fast. I just lifted my hand, fired one round and it hit him in the throat. That was it. He slumped, his arm went down and his finger twitched. He fired into the ground as he spun away and fell."

The commissioner listens, nodding his head.

"I ran over. Kid tried to say something. I don't know what. His throat was just gurgling. Then he closed his eyes, and that was it."

The two men sit in silence. Then the commissioner speaks. "We talked to the younger kid."

"Tony?" Victor asks.

"Right. Tony. Story he told was pretty much the same as yours. We also talked to a woman who was across the street from the mouth of the ally. She saw it unfold too. It's pretty clear from both that you're telling the truth."

Victor sighs and stares at the tiles again. He feels like he should be happy to hear he'll likely be vindicated. He should be feeling something. Anything. But it's like his heart has hardened. Strangely, shooting the boy just feels like a collateral part of basic police business, and that muted empathy seems to bother him the most.

"There will be an official inquiry, of course," the commissioner says. "But I wouldn't worry about it. Far as I'm concerned, the kid was asking for it. He got what he deserved. I'll talk to the people gathered out front. And you should take a couple of days off."

Victor nods.

The commissioner stands to leave the room but turns back. "You know, you did well. Good officers who can keep their head when things turn bad… they're hard to find. We'll do all we can to make sure this blows over. I understand you're only working with us part time right now. By your choice, apparently. But I can tell you, if things stay on track, you are welcome to join us full time. I hope you do."

"I appreciate that, sir. But I'm part time because I have other things going on. I'm even helping with some research for a local university. I must admit, I took this police work when my other job shut down suddenly. But now that's picking up again. I guess I have to make a choice."

The commissioner just pats Victor's shoulder again and heads out the door.

# Chapter 41

## *The Accused*

Amanda blinks as she's led out of her cell and into the bright lights of the stationhouse. She is escorted down a cold hallway. She doesn't realize it, but the trip takes her directly toward Victor Marius who just left his meeting with the commissioner.

But the two never pass.

The police escorting Amanda turn right, moving her swiftly down a side hallway, then into a room with several large windows. Victor continues straight ahead and exits the building.

The big windows offer the first sunlight she's seen in three days.

There's a table in the center of the room. Seated at the table is a police officer and one other man. She can only see the back of his head. When he turns to look at her, Amanda feels as if a block of ice has formed in her stomach. It's the man who was, and still technically is, her husband. Wayne Malcolm.

She closes her eyes and curses him. But the curse is only heard in her mind. She tries to remain stoic in front of the men.

She thought she was heading to an arraignment where she could enter her plea. She was planning to state that she's never tried to kill anyone in her life, and she has no idea why anyone would accuse her of such a thing.

But now she will be confronting a man who will claim to be a victim. Someone who, she guesses, is more than willing to exaggerate to make her look like a criminal. This isn't the way she had expected things to happen when she returned to Boston. She doesn't know Wayne's plan, but she now sees that things could go very wrong for her.

"Is this the woman?" the officer says to Wayne.

"Yes, that's her," he says scornfully.

"And you, ma'am? I assume you know this man?"

Amanda sighs. "Yes. I do."

"Have a seat please."

The policeman spends several minutes, looking through a pile of written notes and telegrams. Amanda and Wayne sit in silence too, avoiding all eye contact with each other.

"Well," the officer sighs, "this is a bit out of the ordinary for me. Usually, we would bring you directly to your arraignment, Mrs. Malcolm, and we'd do everything by the book. But I've taken the liberty of talking to a few people in this matter, and I decided I wanted to discuss things first. With both of you. Together."

He looks at Wayne. "You fully intend to pursue this charge of attempted murder?"

Wayne clenches his teeth and literally growls his answer. "I certainly do."

Then the officer looks at Amanda. "And you maintain your innocence?"

"I don't even know why this charge was filed against me. Attempted murder? That's preposterous."

The officer nods. "That is indeed the charge. Do you have any idea what this could be about?"

Wayne starts to answer. The officer holds his hand up. "I'm asking her."

Amanda closes her eyes. "It's about Wayne getting revenge on me, I suppose. If I had to guess, this is about me defending myself when he was slapping me. That was months ago."

"And you, Mr. Malcolm?"

"She came at me with a knife. Cut me at least twice before I managed to push her away."

"It was a small paring knife, Wayne. I was cutting fruit at the sink when you started slapping me. I simply held the little knife up while I was defending myself. You know that. That's why the scars are only on your hands."

"I think you knew exactly what you were doing!"

The officer sighs. "Will you excuse me for a moment? Just stay here, both of you."

As the officer steps out of the room, he asks a guard at the door to keep an eye on the pair. Once the door closes, the guard does keep watch. But through a small window. Amanda and Wayne find themselves alone and they continue to avoid eye contact.

After a minute of silence, Amanda looks at her husband. "Why are you doing this, Wayne? I don't understand."

"You know very well why I'm doing it. Damn woman!"

"Wayne! You know what happened that day! Yes, I was holding the knife, but I was holding it before you even came in. All I did was block you every time you swung at me!"

"You blatantly stabbed me! My hands and arm were cut."

"I never thrust the knife at you. Not one time."

"That's not what it's about!" Wayne shouts. The guard leans closer to the window as the voice is raised, but he doesn't enter.

"Then what is it about, Wayne? Tell me!"

"It's about respect."

Amanda sits back in her chair, eyes pointed at the ceiling.

"You're right, Wayne. It is. And you never showed me much respect at all."

"I'm talking about *you*, woman. I'm talking about the way you treated me!"

She shakes her head, unable to grasp his point. "I did so much for you, Wayne. So much!"

"Oh, is that what you call it? Your constant push, push, push? Doing? Giving? Are those the words you want to use to explain it all away?"

"What in the world are you talking about?"

"Everything! Every single damn thing! From the crops, to the barn, to the animals. 'Do more, Wayne. Be more, Wayne. I know you can. Give more. Give more and more!'" He looks at her with fire in his eyes.

"I married a poor girl from the city and brought her out to a nice farm. But you couldn't be happy there, could you? No, you wanted more."

Amanda stares at him. "Is that what you're seeking? My gratitude for rescuing me? And then what? I was just supposed to leave you alone in the house to do as you pleased? We were supposed to be a team, Wayne."

He scoffs.

"Like I said, Wayne, I did more for you than you'd like to admit."

"Oh, right. Even in bed. Right? Even there. You *did so much* for me there too—is that what you will claim?"

She looks him in his eyes. "Do you know what really happened, Wayne? After a couple years, you stopped giving me your best. You know you did. You dropped back. I guess that's why I started asking for more. You stopped loving. You stopped trying. You did minimal work."

"That's garbage."

"No, you really did stop trying and you chose to wither instead. In every way. You just stopped everything."

Wayne looks down. "Maybe I did."

"Why? I could never understand that. Why did it happen?"

"Maybe because my best was never good enough."

She shakes her head. "No. I never tried to make you feel that way!"

"Maybe not on purpose. But you did."

She nods slightly, trying to accept this. Or at least his concept of it.

"You didn't want me for what I was, Amanda. You wanted me for what I might be. You wanted me because of where you thought... you might... be able to push me. A man starts to feel the burden of that after a while. Only so much of that a man can take."

"So that was your way of dealing with it? To slap me around?"

"No, no. That's not the way I wanted to deal with it. It's just where things ended up. It was a long, slow slide."

Amanda shakes her head. Then she laughs. "Yes. And look where we've ended up now. A fight that's ending in a lie that may send me to jail. Is that what you want, Wayne?"

Wayne looks at the table. "I just wanted you to feel what I felt. That's why I filed this complaint. I want you to know the hurt. Do you have any feeling of that?"

She blinks. "Of hurt? Yes. I think I might indeed have some idea."

"Then why don't you apologize?"

"What?" she exclaims.

He stares at her, long and hard.

"Apologize for what? For trying to love you and live with you?"

"How about if you apologize for driving me away?" Wayne demands.

Amanda shakes her head and looks toward the wall. For her, the discussion is over.

"Like I said a long time ago," Wayne continues. "People don't know what you really are. There are things you keep hidden, and they come out now and then."

She purses her lips and says nothing.

A minute later, the police officer re-enters the room, sits at the table, and slowly straightens his papers. He keeps it up until he has them all in a perfectly square pile. All eyes are on him, including those of the guard, who has stepped into the room.

"Do either of you have anything to say?"

The response is continued silence.

"I'd like to propose something," the officer says. "I think we can all agree that what happened at your house was not a good thing, but it appears to me that it was far from attempted murder."

Wayne shakes his head. "I don't know why you would say that. In fact, I think—"

The officer holds up his hand. "Mr. Malcolm, at the moment, I don't intend to charge you with anything. Not with violence against your wife. Not with filing a false police report. None of that. But if you don't stay quiet, I can certainly change my mind."

"What?" Wayne shouts with indignation.

The officer looks over at Amanda, who is smiling smugly.

"And as for you, Mrs. Malcolm, or whatever name you are using now...."

"Grant."

"Be quiet! I know your other name, and I know you think this is good news for you, but I'd wipe that grin off your face if I were you. There are any number of things I could still charge you with too."

She blinks in surprise.

"I heard part of your conversation here today. I was listening from the other room. I've also talked privately with your husband. And the one thing that's obvious to me is that he feels you never accepted him. Or worse, that you used him."

"Really? I used him?"

"Married him to get out of your situation. Then pushed him in ways he did not want to go."

"Men!"

She just shakes her head.

"You may feel like you were trying to bring out his best, but I don't think he felt that way at all. As he says, you were never happy with him. Or whatever the heck he said. 'Accepted him for what he was' or something."

"That's right," Wayne adds. "I—"

"God damn it, if you both don't shut up, I'll lock the two of you up for a week!"

Amanda stares at the officer in silence. She tries to listen to what he is saying, but her mind is reeling. How could they think such things about her? How could anyone...?

"I'm sure you are a nice woman, Mrs. Malcolm. I'm sure you are quite capable of bringing out the best in a person. But don't you think you should get that person's agreement first? Without that, you come off as nothing more than a damn shrew."

"That's right," Wayne adds. The officer flings the pile of papers at him.

Then, he points at both of them, first at Wayne and then at Amanda. "Look, both of you. Here's what I propose. Mr. Malcolm, I propose that you drop the charges. But before you do, I'd like to hear your wife apologize to you. For everything. I agree with that much."

"What!" Amanda says. "That's preposterous. Why I—"

"Do you want to rot in jail, lady?" Then he turns to Wayne. "And if you drop the charges and make your own apology, I promise that I won't charge you with anything either, including wife abuse."

Wayne literally shakes in anger.

"I mean it! An apology from both of you. Then I want you out of here!" The officer raises his voice. Wayne can see the seriousness in his face, and he slowly nods. "Yeah, maybe. But that's if she apologizes first."

Amanda seethes, "Apologize? Why, you can just go to—"

"Lady," the cop interrupts, "I'm a busy man. You've got one shot at this."

"Fine," she says, her nose wrinkled. "I'm sorry, Wayne. Sorry I pushed you so. Whether you believe it or not, I really was happy in the beginning. About some things. Well, a lot of things really. I liked the farm. And the animals. And often even you. I'm sorry for whatever I did that made us lose all of that."

The cop stares at her husband. "Fair enough? Charges dropped?"

Wayne shrugs.

"Answer the damn question!"

"All right! Fair enough. I withdraw the complaint."

The cop nods. "And now, Mr. Malcolm. I'd like you to apologize to your wife too."

"I'm not going to do that!"

"I might have said I wasn't going to charge you, Mr. Malcolm. But I'm certainly within my rights to keep you right here at this table for as long as it takes to investigate this situation. And if that takes all night, you can just sit here."

"Fine. To hell with it. I'll say my apology, but only because you're making me. That's all. I'm sorry, okay? I'm sorry!"

The officer gives a slight shrug and looks over at Amanda.

There's a long moment of silence, then both the cop and Amanda are surprised to hear Wayne add, in a low voice, "I'm … I'm sorry for everything. I really am." He blinks several times. And looks away.

With that, the officer nods to the guard, and the door is opened. Wayne stands, looks back over his shoulder one last time at Amanda. Then he walks out. There's deep hurt in both of their eyes.

"You're free to go," the officer says to Amanda. "I'll have someone bring your things. I think you were carrying some kind of sack with a box in it? Plus a billfold with a little money."

Walking out the door, he sees the youngest cop in the precinct who had been listening at the door.

"That … that was mighty impressive, sir."

"Yeah, well, the police work isn't always what you think it is, kid. Sometimes it's just about playing referee."

A few minutes later, a jail matron brings Amanda the sack and she heads toward the stationhouse door.

"One of our patrolmen can use a wagon to drop you where you need to go," the matron says.

"That would be nice. There's a place that makes boilers. It's just a few blocks from here. He can drop me there. I need to pick up something that belongs to me."

## Chapter 42

*Florence*

The telegram sits on a workbench, just a few inches from Victor's left hand. He looks over at it. Picks it up. Rereads it, then carefully sets it down again. He tries to decide what to make of the message. In the meantime, he continues his work, and waits for the knock at the door.

The telegram arrived about 90 minutes ago. It contained just a few words, but for some reason, the words have stirred deep emotions in him.

VICTOR.
I HEARD WHAT HAPPENED. [STOP]
I'M SO SORRY – YOU MUST BE DEVASTATED [STOP]
I WOULD LIKE TO COME SEE YOU TODAY. LATE MORNING [STOP]
- FLORENCE

That's a name he did not expect to see again. Nor did he expect to ever see Florence face to face again, nor talk to her.

Yet, now she's on her way. Victor does feel a little sense of excitement.

When the knock comes on the lab's heavy door, he stands up, takes a deep breath, and wipes his hands on a rag.

He swings the door wide, and there she stands. As lovely as ever. Burgundy taffeta dress. Silver broad-brim hat. And those dark curls. That bright smile.

In Florence's world, it's a breach of etiquette for her to come visit him without an escort. But it somehow seems appropriate to him. She's come to – what? To comfort? To offer sympathy and understanding?

Today, it does seem like a very private conversation is best. Their eyes meet. Their gazes linger.

"Hello, Victor."

He nods. "Florence... good to see you."

She extends her hand, he gives it a quick kiss, then stands awkwardly, like a boy lost in the woods. She leans in and gives him a solid hug.

"May I come in?"

"Oh, of course. Yes, please!"

As she enters, Victor realizes he's not used to having a woman in the building. The crates and boards that serve as seating for other visitors don't seem at all appropriate for Florence. He remembers that there's a pair of padded and embroidered folding chairs stashed in a corner. He claimed them from a trash heap when a nearby theater was being renovated. He sets up the chairs in the middle of the room and offers her a glass of water.

"I must say, Florence, I was surprised to get your telegram."

"Were you?" She responds. "I know my father talked to you. I know you told him it was up to me to reach out to you. Seemed a bit pouty on your part, no?" She winks, and he feels his heart melt a bit. "But I do understand."

"Thank you for that. But that conversation with your father was many days ago. I had assumed you were not in favor of my terms."

Florence nods. "Well, I was not. But then..."

"But then you heard. About the shooting."

"Yes. In all the newspapers. Oh, Victor, I am so sorry. What a fright. I feel badly for the poor boy, of course. But I also feel badly for you. You certainly are not a violent or vindictive person. The Boston Evening Transcript was critical of what happened, but all the other reports said it came down to you or the boy. And most of the stories said more than that – that you may have been protecting another boy? I can see you making that choice. And I'm sure it was not an easy one."

Victor looks into the distance. "No. It was not. But I'm trying to believe I made the right choice. I guess I have to think that."

Florence nods. "I guess that's just part of policing. Not that I know anything at all about that world."

Victor rises and walks to the window. He stares out but doesn't really see anything. "I didn't know much of this world either. But I've learned. And now I have to decide if I want to stay."

"Do you think you will?"

He shrugs.

"Could you do good if you stayed? Or will it wear you down? My father has told me about policemen he's known. He said some grow hard. Cold inside. Everything and everyone becomes suspicious. They stop trusting people. People stop trusting them. I guess that's what happens when you deal with the worst people every day. I would hate to see that happen to you."

Victor lets out a slow breath. "You know, I'm less worried about that, than about finding myself in the same situation again. I don't know if I could handle that one more time. There is no joy in pulling a trigger. I don't know if I would make the same choice a second time." He takes another deep breath. "I don't want to see that again up close."

"You don't want to see someone dying?"

"More than that. I don't want to see their faces. That's what I remember the most. The look on that boy's face right after I shot. The shot made him stumble back, and right before he fell, he looked down at the blood spilling from his neck onto his chest. Then he looked up at me. And he knew he was done. His face was pure pain."

Florence closes her eyes.

Victor's voice wavers. " I don't mean just the pain of the bullet, which I'm sure was bad. I mean the pain of where he found himself in that moment. The bad family life that sent him to the orphanage. The bad choices he made after that. The circumstances of his life put him on a sad road from the start. Then he suddenly saw it ending. He was a dirt-poor kid who did what he thought he had to do. Those choices cost him. I could tell he realized that. Yet, what other path could he have followed? His was a life of very limited choices."

"I suppose that's quite true."

"And why…" Victor looks at her, "why did I have to be the one to end it? Why was I the one who got to see that all, up close?"

He presses his fingers to his forehead. So far, he has blocked all emotions related to that day. He's been stoic, tough and resigned, just like a police officer should be. But now, Florence has come, and he's suddenly thinking way too much about these things. And about her..."

He hears her rise from her chair and approach him. "It's all right, Victor. That's why I wanted to come. It's all right, darling."

He turns to her, says nothing, but welcomes her embrace. That wonderful breath. The slim shoulder lurking beneath its lovely dark fabric. He doesn't want any tears to fall onto that dress. But they do.

"Why? Why did he..." But that's all he says before he buries his face in Florence's hair and the nape of her neck. And the emotion comes like a wave.

Victor knows right then – he's glad she came.

# Chapter 43

## *Fired Up*

"What do you mean I can't take it?" Amanda says. "It's my wagon. I've changed my mind, and I want to take it out of here."

The owner of the Eastside Boilerworks Company looks adamant in his opposition.

"But you asked me to sell it, and I did. Somebody left a deposit. You can't just come back here and cancel our deal. I have his money!"

Amanda tries to look equally unyielding. "Well, I'm not able to sell it anymore. I need it. You can just go ahead and give that person their deposit back. Tell them I'm sorry."

The boilermaker shakes his head. "Oh lady, what are you doing? Why did you come in here and waste my time?"

"I didn't mean to," she says. "It's just that plans have changed. I can pay you for storage. I mean… I think."

The owner goes back into his shop while Amanda starts to shovel coal into the wagon's firebox. It will take the usual long time to get the wagon's boiler up to steam. While she's working, the owner of the shop sends his assistant out the back door. The boilermaker does not want to lose his commission, so he has the young man run up the street, carrying a note.

Jeb had asked to be notified immediately if the owner came back and tried to move the cart, so the message is on its way.

Amanda continues to pop pieces of coal into the fire, blowing on them as she does so. It takes a maddeningly long time to get the wagon ready to move.

"I can't imagine," she says to herself while lying on her belly and blowing on the coals, "why anyone would think self-propelled vehicles will someday replace horses. I just don't see it. If I owned a horse, I'd be blocks away by now."

She gets a very low boil going, but the pressure gauge barely registers. It's only crept up a few more clicks by the time Jeb Thomas and Devlin Richards, having read the note, rush to the side of a nearby brick building. They peer around the corner.

"There she is," Devlin says. "Just like you predicted. She's come back for it, and she's got that damn sack with her. Would you look at that!"

Jeb nods. "Oh yes. This is perfect. Let's just stroll up there and—"

"No. She'll make a fuss. Draw attention."

Jeb reconsiders. "Then maybe we can just quietly climb aboard when she starts to pull out of the shop?"

Devlin sneers. "I think we can do more than that." He takes the stolen police revolver out of his pocket, checks the cylinders, then tucks the weapon under his coat, still gripping the handle.

"Hold on," Jeb says. "The idea is to jump aboard the cart and then hang on until we take the box from her. That's all."

"We're doing what we need to do," Devlin says. "I ain't planning to shoot. But this is our insurance. This time, she's not getting away."

Amanda puts more coal into the fire box, then closes the door. She sits in the seat and moves one of the levers. When it looks like the wagon is finally starting to move, Devlin starts moving too – staying low. Following along behind it. Jeb joins the line. The noise of the engine drowns out any sounds they make.

Then Jeb sees the southerner cock the pistol's hammer.

"What are you doing, Richards?" he whispers loudly. "This wasn't part of the plan. You don't need to—"

Devlin spins around and points the gun at Jeb. "You know what your problem is, Thomas? You ain't got the guts to do what needs to be done. You talk a good game, but when it comes down to it, you're yellow. You're a damn coward about some things, you know that? Like this here. You're just a Yankee polecat!"

"Oh, so you're the hardened one? You and I have both killed people." Jeb fires back. "Doesn't prove a thing. Today's not supposed to be about killing."

"Yeah? Let me tell you what today *is* actually about. If we take that box from her, we leave a witness. And if I'm caught, they've got a whole bunch of other things to charge me with. To charge *us* with. Got it? I ain't going to get caught, and I sure as hell ain't going to let that box slip away."

Jeb looks anxious. Angry. "You can't just shoot her!"

"Only reason I don't shoot you first is that would spook her. Now you just get the hell out of here if you don't want to be part of this. We'll make her drive us outside of town. Then I'm finishing things... that's a damn fact."

When Devlin turns to rush down the street, Jeb loses his temper. He lacks a weapon, so closes in and hits Devlin in the head with both fists, then tackles him to the ground. The gun clatters to the street. Jeb continues with his punches, throwing his full weight behind them.

"Amanda! Go! Now!" he yells.

She barely hears his voice above the hiss of steam. When she looks back over her shoulder, her eyes widen.

Jeb and Devlin roll over and over in the street, punching and kicking at each other. Amanda sees their deadly fight. She turns and sees the boilermaker coming towards her.

"I'm sorry. Here!" She throws some coins. "This should cover your trouble. I have to move!"

Pulling hard on the big lever to increase her speed, she hears the wagon groan. The gears mesh and the rig speeds out of the shop yard. But a horse and carriage block the direction she wants to go.

She can see Devlin has risen to his feet now, and he's kicking hard at Jeb's ribcage.

She turns about and starts to steer to the right, then decides to veer to the left instead. She bears down on the two fighting men. Pulling the lever all the way back, she rockets forward, aiming directly at Devlin. In shock and surprise, he looks up, then dives mostly out of the way. She barely grazes him, but it's enough to send him tumbling onto the gravel.

Jeb, bloody around his mouth and holding his sides in pain, stumbles to his feet. He sees Devlin's gun on the ground and staggers over to pick it up. He points it at Devlin. The southerner is up, running lightning fast. He zigs, then zags. Jeb fires again and again as Devlin bolts down the street, disappearing into the distance.

As Jeb empties the last of the pistol's chambers, a pair of police officers arrive. Immediately one of them grabs Jeb's hand, wrenching the gun free. The other cop slams Jeb against the wall and begins to frisk.

"Well, look what we have here," says the cop holding the gun. "This is a police pistol."

"That's not mine."

"Boston mark on it. I'll wager I know exactly who this one belonged to." He shows it to the other officer. "How about that, Irv? We may have caught our cop killer."

"No," Jeb says through bloody lips. "You've got it all wrong. I just picked it up. I'm telling you—it isn't mine!"

# Chapter 44

## *Climbing and Testing*

The climb up a utility pole is not a long one. But Victor has made the trip five times in the last hour, and he feels it in his legs. Each time he climbs, it's to check the work of his men. He sometimes makes adjustments to wire connections. And he occasionally climbs to mount his antenna as he searches for Professor Alton's signal.

*Something's wrong.*

He should have picked up the next signal by now. He should have heard something. A *tap tap tap* like a woodpecker. Yet there's been nothing but static. It's frustrating. He feels, once again, like he's wasting his time.

At the top of each hour, the professor is supposed to send out a signal. Each signal is to be issued at a slightly different frequency and each test is supposed to last about ten minutes, giving Victor a chance to set his antenna, listen, and make adjustments if needed.

But after an afternoon of ill-fated attempts, he's stymied. "Broad-spectrum receiver indeed," Victor mumbles as he climbs down. He drops his wrench into the grass and collapses into a shady spot beside the road. Why isn't this working? Is the problem at this end, or on the broadcast end?

Part of him wants to tear the antenna down and concentrate on his real job of running wires.

They have one more test scheduled for the day. Fifty minutes from now. He walks down the street to a small store and buys a big jug of lemonade for his crew. He eyes the wine and the beer longingly. But so far, on this work assignment, he's avoided drinking, and he'll continue that avoidance.

At the top of the hour—the last hour and the last test of the day—he climbs the pole once more, sets up his antenna and small receiver, and waits, the weight of his body suspended from a long leather utility belt.

He dons a set of headphones. Again, he hears nothing. He adjusts two screws. Still nothing. After a third adjustment, he stops. He places his hand to his ear. At first, he thinks it's just raw background noise. Or maybe a distant chugging train, or a woodpecker. Then he smiles. No. this is the signal he's been searching for. It's very distant. Much weaker than he thought it would be, but there it is. Seven taps. Then a rest, then seven more.

He braces himself against the pole and makes notes, writing down the exact frequency, time, and other measures. He makes several adjustments to the system's settings. With each adjustment, the signal grows louder. By the time the test ends, he can hear the signal quite clearly. This time, his climb down feels weightless. This success boosts his energy and lifts his spirits.

He slaps a couple of his men on the back, never mentioning the radio tests, but making sure all the workers know they've had a good day in the field.

He asks if anyone knows where he might be able to send a telegram, but he gets nothing but blank stares. Eventually he learns from a passing farmer that the nearest office is over ten miles away. Notifying Alton of this success will have to wait.

Later, in his tent, Victor's sleep is restless. He dreams of hearing nothing from the radio ever again. He dreams of searching every day, and never finding.

Then his head is filled with static, then thoughts of falling from a power pole, and then from a much higher tower. He dreams of his lab burning to the ground. Through it all, there is a steady *click click click* in the background. It's only at the end of his dream that he realizes noise is the signal he's been searching for all along.

The next morning, again at the prescribed time, he installs his antenna and plugs in again. This time, the signal is stronger. Per arrangement with the professor, he also tries to listen in on three other frequencies, and he gets two of them to work. It's a fantastic success for the day.

Two days later, he finds that he doesn't need to send a cable to the professor. The old man has come out to see him and the work crew by riding a horse along the path of new wires – for miles.

Victor runs to congratulate the old man, and to share details of the success. "You know," Victor laughs, "for the first time since that shipwreck, I feel like I'm back on track. I'm back where I want to be."

"So, you'll run more tests with me next week?"

"Yes. Yes, of course. And you need to start sending me longer messages."

"And the weeks after? For the next few months? We have scads of work to do, Victor! So much to test and understand."

Victor's face droops suddenly. "I don't.... I mean... I can't. At least not every day. Not at this level."

The reality of his situation sinks in. Radio research has been little more than his hobby for many months. He'd love to commit every moment of his time to it. But he doesn't have the freedom nor the money. He still must work, and if he doesn't keep his job, he'll lose what little income he has.

With no great benefactor looking to fund their research, he and the professor can't sustain this level of work on their own.

"I can work through next week," he tells his friend. "But the power company is sending me up into New Hampshire the week after that. I've also decided, after the shooting, to put my police work on hold for a while. I have a chance to manage these installations full time again. We'll be running wires to three cities!"

"For how long?" the professor demands. He's obviously irritated at the interruption.

"Probably a few months into the winter, until the ground gets too hard to set the new poles. I'll be managing multiple line crews. I don't even know where I'll be staying. I think they expect us to keep living in tents, for God's sake."

"Will you return on weekends?"

"Maybe on occasion. But the company won't pay my train fare if I do. I don't think I'll be back very often, professor."

Professor Alton looks terribly disappointed. They discuss when they might meet again.

"Listen," Alton confides, "I do think it's important that we try to get you some funding so you can stay in Boston. You know, I want to bring you on board as a professor and to take us to the next round of research. So, for now, go. Do your job. I'll handle the paperwork. But I'm not going to do everything for free, lad. I expect to own a piece of this company, whatever it turns out to be after we get our radio equipment design hammered out and into manufacturing. Until then, I'll keep you in the know – any way that I can."

Victor smiles. "Yes. That's fine. I'd be proud to work with you."

By the end of the next day, the work crew is a few miles from where the successful radio test was conducted. Victor rides the extra distance to find the telegraph office. He sends a message to Tesla, telling of his great success with their latest radio tests.

A reply comes the next day, congratulating him, and taking part of the credit for putting some of the ideas in Victor's head.

Tesla asks where he is now and informs Victor to be on the lookout for a thick envelope that's on its way to his closest post office —with a little surprise.

Victor can't pick up the delivery for several days. When he does, he finds a fat brown envelope, and inside he finds a note from Tesla.

*My dear lad, I thought you might like to know that a beautiful woman stopped by my apartment recently. She inquired about you. She apparently thought you were dead, and she wanted to learn as much information about you as she could.*

This puzzles Victor, since he knows virtually no one besides Tesla in New York. Why would a woman look for him there, and why did she think he was deceased?

He reads on.

*This woman, who said her name is Amanda Grant, told me about finding your diary. She said it had washed up on the Cape Cod seashore, in some kind of peculiar box. She read the diary, and in the part that describes your research, apparently my name was mentioned. That's why she came to see me.*

Victor's legs suddenly feel weak. He sits down and rereads the letter. Is this true? This woman found his puzzle box? He had never expected to hear about that box or its contents again.

His next thought is – *it did its job.*

He shakes his head, dumbfounded.

The box did its job. It floated up. It bobbed and rode the waves all the way back to land. But what does that mean? If this woman found the diary, that means she also found the whole puzzle box and its contents. Victor laughs to himself. So, the old sailor's legends were true! If the box survives, people will notice it. They will find what's inside if they can get it open.

He reads one more line from Tesla's note.

*I told her that you are very much alive. She seemed shocked. Then excited.*

In his mind, Victor replays his terrible struggle on the sinking ship. The memories bring a deep chill. He remembers escaping. But even more, he remembers the terror. His final few memories include a point where he found himself accepting that it was his time to die. That point came as he was releasing the box through one of the Gossamer's portholes. He remembers the sight of it rising toward the surface as he and the ship slowly dropped deeper into the bluish gray. The recollection makes him shiver again.

So, who is this woman who found his puzzle box? She obviously figured out how to get some of it open. Does that mean she opened and found everything? She is obviously smart enough that she figured out how to find Tesla.

Victor also thinks about the diamonds. *His* diamonds.

In the bottom level of the box.

Real ones.

Most people, if they found such riches, would keep their mouths shut. So why wouldn't she avoid meeting the very person who could possibly reclaim them? Wouldn't she want to keep them as her own?

Or maybe she didn't find the whole box. Maybe it broke apart, and she only found the diary.

The idea that she's read his personal thoughts embarrasses him. His innermost feelings, hopes, and dreams were scrawled in that small book. He's not even sure why he tossed it into the box at the last moment.

Victor realizes there's something else in the envelope besides Tesla's letter. At first, Victor thinks it's his own journal being returned to him.

But the item he pulls out doesn't look like his journal at all. It's a different book entirely.

It's someone else's diary.

Scrawled across its cover, in pencil, is a note in a woman's handwriting. Drawing his finger over it, he reads the words out loud.

*Dear Victor. I very much enjoyed reading your journal. You have some very progressive thoughts and hopes. It would be quite interesting to discuss these with you. Perhaps someday we can do that, now that I know you are alive.*

*Since turnabout is fair play, I thought I should give you a look at my diary too. I've asked Mr. Telsa to hold onto my notebook, and once he figures out where you are, I've asked him to send it along with his letter. I started this diary fairly recently, and I don't think my experiences are nearly as worldly as yours. But I want you to know that you helped inspire me to make a journey of my own. I thank you for that.*

*Sincerely, Amanda Grant.*

Victor sits with a mouth-half-open sort of smile. It's the boastful smile of a man who has discovered someone, somewhere, might care about what he did, what he thinks, and what he marked down on paper. And now, this other person, this courageous woman, has decided to share her own thoughts with him.

He reads Amanda's diary far into the night and takes it with him on the Portsmouth-bound train in the morning. Through it all, his smile barely wanes.

# Chapter 45

## *Amanda Says*

Victor reaches the last page of Amanda's journal. He has enjoyed the story so much that he hesitates to read the final lines. He doesn't want that tale to end.

So, he stops, and reviews what he has learned so far about this young woman.

The poor neighborhood where she grew up

The marriage that didn't last, and its furious, confounding end.

Her escape that took her back to Boston and then across the country. Then her sense of sad failure and loss, leading to a tough but cathartic trip home.

And apparently, Victor was there in spirit – to accompany her in her darkest moments. He had no idea.

As someone who had his own harrowing escapes and personal trials, he recognizes toughness and determination when he sees it. He takes a deep breath and decides to read the end of her tale. As he turns the last page, something falls out. It's a photograph.

Tintype. Stamp on the back from a Boston photo studio. A date written next to the stamp says it was taken in June.

He sees an image of a lovely woman. Long dark hair pulled back in a ribbon. Soft curls. Impish smile. He is mesmerized. He studies it for several minutes and the view continues to draw him in.

Eventually his eyes return to the book, and he reads the final paragraphs.

*So, Victor, I thank you for taking the time to read this diary. I have no idea where you are, and I have no idea if you will ever get this book. But I hope you do. If you would ever like to meet, I would be honored to do so.*

*Of course, I have no idea where you are. And I can't tell you where I might be, because my life is in flux. But I know we are both in Boston, or at least somewhere in New England. I will look for you. I hope you will do the same.*

Victor goes back to work, but the thought of Amanda, wherever she may be, doesn't leave his mind. He's not sure what it all means. But he finds it fascinating, and he feels more alive than he has in weeks.

# Chapter 46

## *Father*

A few days later, Victor is back in Boston and back in his police uniform. He's walking back to his residence, when an ornate carriage pulls up. He knows immediately who it is. He nods hello to Howard Gatwick, Florence's father.

Seated behind the driver, the old man taps the seat next to him, but Victor declines his offer to climb aboard. Instead, he rests his foot on the step board below the side door. "Hello, Howard. Beautiful day, isn't it?"

"It's quite a delightful day, Victor. It's only two in the afternoon and I've already traded a stock that gained me nearly a thousand dollars." He smiles. "Nothing brightens one's outlook more than a successful bit of business."

Victor nods. "I imagine that's true. So, what brings you here, sir?

"I understand that Florence has been around to visit you. Yes? She said the two of you had a nice conversation. That's splendid."

"Yes, we saw each other, and yes, the conversation was nice."

The old man smiles. "Nice enough that we may see you around the house again?"

Victor doesn't respond.

"She misses you, you know. There have been other visitors. They don't seem to strike her fancy. Mine either, truth be told. Vultures, some of them. They smell beauty and money and they try to charm her and myself." He looks Victor in the eye. "You were different. I appreciated that. I've told you, Victor, you would make a good addition to our team, but frankly, I'm not one to chase you or anyone. And I wouldn't do it, if it wasn't for..."

"For her?"

"Yes. Exactly. It's just the two of us, you know. Florence and me. She brightens the place. She is the true warmth of my small family. If she is forlorn, the whole nature of the house changes. So, yes, she is why I am here."

"But you are still looking for me to join your business."

"I am. But it's not a strict rule. I've told you as much."

Victor nods. "Truth be told, sir, the rule seems stricter for her. You have given her quite a life. It's clear to me she wants someone who can step in and keep her in that level of splendor. And that is the problem."

"I have no doubt that you could, Victor. I can see to that."

"Thank you. As I've said, I have a job."

"Yes, yes. I see the uniform. How is that police salary working for you? You're walking on your rounds, Victor. Can't they even give you a horse? Or perhaps I should loan you one?"

"Actually, sir, my police work will be waning. I hope to start to teach soon. In the meantime, I'm spending more time than ever doing my electrical lineman work. I may work both jobs for a while. Save up a little money."

"A teacher? Really?"

"Yes. At MIT. Assistant professor of Physics."

"My goodness. Well, good for you."

Victor steps back from the carriage.

"I appreciate your candor, Mr. Gatwick."

"Please, call me Howard."

"Of course." Victor smiles politely. "And you should know, I've never actually said no to Florence. How could I? She's overwhelmingly charming." That causes both to laugh.

"But what I did do," Victor continues, "was to set my terms. And that has caused her to go quiet. Any relationship is about two futures, right? So, with her, is it love? Or am I a business transaction? And she is stubborn. And I know that's because she learned all of that from the best."

Howard Gatwick chuckles. "I think maybe I'll consider that a compliment, Victor, and leave it at that."

The two men nod. Howard's driver snaps the reigns, and the coach pulls away from the curb.

# Chapter 47

## *North Shore*

As she heads toward the northern outskirts of the city, the number of horses and carriages on the road drops to almost nothing. A wider road beckons. Amanda opens a valve on the old Dudgeon wagon and instantly feels the acceleration as more steam is channeled to the two big pistons. As the clunking and hissing drives the rear wheels, her speed doubles. She wears no hat, and her hair whips wildly in the wind.

A pedestrian stops, stares, and waves as she rockets past. She waves back, and the wave helps spark a broad smile on her face – because Amanda again feels resilient and capable. Almost invincible. Does anyone ever really appreciate a capable woman? Wayne certainly never…

*Stop.*

She shakes the thought away. *Just stop.* Wayne does not need to occupy her mind anymore. Not for another moment.

But she does think of others. Jonathan Morgan for instance. She could always feel his quiet admiration. He was totally unthreatened by her. He was a good mentor. His wife, on the other hand, was not. Sometimes it's other women who most fear a strong woman. Amanda doesn't understand this.

She turns her attention to the road. She has a rough idea of where she's heading – past Revere and Lynn and Salem. She knows that one big bucket of anthracite coal will move the steam wagon about 13 miles. Less if she's climbing hills. After her last stop, she now has the equivalent of 11 buckets on board. If she adds an occasional chunk of dry wood, she should have enough fuel to reach well into New Hampshire.

Her plan is to retreat to a small hunting camp Jonathan told her about. Summer season is over now, and the traditional fall hunting season has yet to begin. So, Amanda figures that will be a good place to hide in for a while. She hasn't mentioned this destination to a soul, including Jonathan Morgan.

No word will get back to Jeb or anyone.

*Jeb... is he still alive? Did he survive that savage beating?*
*Oh, Jeb. She shakes her head. ... How did things go so wrong?*

She adjusts a knob and kicks a few more coals onto the fire. A slight smile reaches her face as she rushes north on hissing steam and iron-clad wheels.

After passing the village of Newburyport and turning northwest a bit, she heads through a series of small villages. A narrower road takes her across the New Hampshire border. In less than an hour, she reaches a town called Kingston. The hunting camp sits on the outskirts of the town.

Dirt path near a big willow. That's what Jonathan said. Eventually she finds it.

The camp has tents pitched on top of short wooden platforms. She also finds a couple of cabins that are nicer than she expected. One even has screens on the windows. There's a good supply of wood stacked next to a woodstove, and enough potted meat and jars of preserves in the pantry to last for several days.

But the best part is the beautiful view of a stream that leads out to a wide river. The anticipation of this view is one of the things that brought her here. Jonathan told stories about the incredible peace and serenity he found here. He said sometimes he would come up here to hunt, then he'd barely hunt at all. Instead, he would sit and watch the deer and the geese and he would just absorb the tranquility.

She takes to the quiet camp life quickly. She stacks more firewood, catches a fish with one of the camp's poles, and tidies up the place, even finding an old curtain to serve as a tablecloth. It's too bad the camp doesn't have electricity.

After supper on her second day, she sits on a bentwood rocker in front of her hut. The evening is warm enough. She pulls the puzzle box out of its sack, and in the day's waning gold light, she turns it over and over in her hands. A chipmunk, probably tamed and fed by previous camp residents, climbs onto the table next to her, begging for crumbs.

Amanda quickly opens multiple levels of the box, right down to the level containing the radio coil. Then she looks to see how she might open the next level. She is sure that's the final level.

After a few minutes of pushing and examining, she blinks in astonishment. It might be the yellow lighting. Or maybe the box, having been banged around in recent days, is showing signs of stress. But she can now see a slight seam near the middle of the bottom compartment. She hasn't noticed it before. She goes inside the cabin to find a hunting knife.

The crack is slightly bigger at one end. When she slides the blade in there, she hears a metallic click. Nothing happens. Tugging does nothing. The box stays firm.

Turning it over, she sees a sliver of copper, maybe a half inch long, protruding from the bottom. That wasn't there before. She must have somehow released it with the knife. It looks like a small piece of a nail pounded flat. Victor's design? On a hunch, she yanks the flat sliver out and feels the whole bottom inch of the box shift.

With a little effort, she's able to spin the teakwood addition off from the base of the original main box. The seam blended so well it was nearly invisible until today.

She carefully opens the compartment, squinting and a bit nervous.

When she fully opens her eyes, she gasps in wonder at the sight before her.

*My God, this explains the rattle in the box.*

It also explains why so many people wanted to get their hands on it. The last rays of sunlight seem to amplify everything inside the tray. The light strikes many, many cut facets, creating a warm glow.

Amanda stares at a shining pile of diamonds. Even electric lights do not shine so brilliantly.

She takes a quick breath. She covers the tray and looks around. No one is here but her. She looks again, then reaches out to touch. Then she holds one stone up for examination.

Yes, they really are diamonds. But how? Her heart races.

Dozens of them. No... even more. Over 80. Maybe even ninety! Large and small. Mostly white but a few with lovely hues of blue or gray. She takes an instant like to the ones with the otherworldly colors, admiring their splendid imperfections.

And in that moment, she realizes her troubles are solved. Not today or tomorrow. But this windfall could help her find her way out of this mess. She suspects these stones hold more value than what she and Wayne would have ever earned by working their farm for the next few years.

"Oh my. Thank God. And thank you, Victor, wherever you are."

And with that, her feeling of relief is replaced by a pang of guilt. If Victor is indeed still alive, these jewels belong to him, not her. She should return them, and not use them to buy her own freedom and safety.

She bites her lip and looks out over the creek for a long time.

By the time the sun has fully set, she starts to smile.

Tesla's notes and drawings will help her connect the dots to find the elusive Victor. She vows to return the diamonds to him if she can. But he will have to find her, and she will have to use a few of the diamonds to help make that easier for him.

Shooing the chipmunk away, she pours the stones onto the table and counts them. There are ninety-one in all. At least thirty of them appear to be well over one carat in size. Six of them look like they're over two! There are a handful that appear to be much larger.

Should she try to sell the larger ones first, or last?

*Sometimes life is but a series of looming tragedies, trying their best not to unfold.* That's what she told herself back in June.

But occasionally life also holds pleasant surprises. This is one of those times.

A week later, she's consumed most of the food in the hunting camp's pantry. By visiting a women's clothing store in a nearby town, she managed to sell two of the smaller stones.

When she makes her way to a general store to buy new provisions, she realizes she's become the talk of the town. Who is this woman who drives herself in a noisy, hissing steam machine? Why does she have diamonds to sell? And the strangest thing of all, why has she been asking questions about where she might buy an electric generator?

Word gets around, not only in this town, but to other small stores and trading posts along a route. Devlin Richards knows Amanda escaped in the general direction of New Hampshire. So, he followed to that area, and offered money to delivery drivers who ply the local routes. Most of them help supply general stores between Boston and Manchester. Figuring she would eventually have to emerge from hiding to look for food, Devlin's idea was simple. He requested that the drivers ask the store owners if any of them saw a woman and a steam car.

Eventually, one of the drivers sees Devlin again and offers an update. Yes, there is such a woman. And she was not at all hard to notice. She's been seen in town more than once.

Now Devlin can narrow her location down to a few miles.

He is also told that the woman has been asking store owners where she might be able to buy a generator. He's not sure what that's about, but he doesn't care. He gives the driver some coins and sets out for a long ride on his stolen horse.

# Chapter 48

## Messages in the Medium

*I feel strong now. Very strong,* Victor thinks to himself as he climbs up his fourteenth utility pole of the day. His mind goes back to when he didn't feel so healthy. After the shipwreck. After his body was battered. After it withered and he had to work to rebuild himself.

Today, months later, his legs feel like steel. Even his shoulders and forearms have grown and hardened with the physical effort of hauling wires and insulators up the poles. Plus, he's eating like a horse.

The wire crew has traveled so far from home that they seldom return to Boston, or even Massachusetts. They live in their tents and bring the electricity with them as they move down the roads.

Sleeping outdoors has become chilly as the weeks move into fall. But at least the power company has been providing great food. Eggs, beef jerky, cans of beans. They even send mason jars full of fruits on occasion. When his men are well fed, Victor hears few complaints.

He's also having great luck with his radio tests. By constantly tweaking the signal, he and Professor Alton have managed to communicate from farther and farther apart. They test it at least twice per day. Victor currently has his portable antenna set up over seventy miles from Boston. The signal is weaker, but he can still find it. Their Morse code communication remains one-way, since Victor can't answer. But the professor sends ideas on how to change configurations and improve reception.

On his fifth day in New Hampshire, Victor receives an urgent message from Professor Alton. The dots and dashes arrive in quick bursts, and Victor can tell the old man is excited about something. Victor writes the letters down. There are no pauses or [STOP]s between the sentences and he struggles to keep up with the incoming blips.

VICTOR FOUND POSSIBLE INVESTOR NEED TO HAVE YOU VISIT MAYBE NEXT WEEK CONFIRM PLEASE I HAVE NO IDEA HOW WE CAN MANUFACTURE THIS EQUIPMENT BUT THAT IS WHAT THEY SEEK LET'S FIGURE OUT HOW TO LAUNCH THIS

He pictures Professor Alton scurrying around the city, visiting investors, and putting business deals together. If Victor manages to live until an old age, he hopes he'll live his life the same way. Still plugging away at new ideas and enjoying the excitement of building something new and incredible.

# Chapter 49

## *Brown Paper*

Thanks to the contacts he's made at The Rose Point, Devlin has been able to recruit two rough, experienced men to ride with him. They head north out of the city. The promised wages are five dollars per day plus a percentage of whatever they're able to take from Amanda. He hired the pair because they both have horses, and a history of taking what they want from people.

The trio head over the New Hampshire border and toward Manchester. As they get closer, they veer off and point their horses toward a store called Miller's Mercantile.

When they arrive, Devlin doesn't go inside. Instead, he visits a blacksmith's barn and some other shops. He directs his questions to them. But he gets his first real answer from a man on the street.

"Oh, that woman?" A man near an apothecary responds. "Yes, I've seen her. Certainly heard her loud wagon. Why?"

He beckons the man closer, whispering low so that no one, not even his hired men, will hear the rest of the conversation.

"She stole some things from me" is Devlin's reply.

"Oh yeah? She didn't steal diamonds by any chance, did she?"

Devlin's eyes narrow to thin slits. The man wonders if he's said the wrong thing. He looks at Devlin nervously, and notices the frightening scar on his cheek.

Devlin spits tobacco juice onto the floor. "Yeah. She stole diamonds. That's right. How the hell did you know that?"

The man starts to back away, choosing to limit his involvement. "Well, I never actually seen those diamonds myself, you understand. But I hear tell that she was offering one or two of them diamonds around several days ago. Looking for a buyer. That's all. And I never really seen her except when she was driving through."

"Which direction was she coming from?"

The man points south. She did some errands here in the village, then drove back that same way."

"That all you know? Think, damn it!" Devlin says with a growl.

The man looks genuinely perplexed. "Well, someone told me when she heads away, she always turns off at the old campground road by the pond. That's about a mile. There's a big willow next to the turn. But I don't know for sure that she goes that way. It's just talk."

Devlin grabs the man's arm to stop his retreat. He pulls a brown piece of paper from his pocket. "Show me," he commands. "Draw a map that shows how to get there from here! Tell me what's on that road."

The man makes a hasty sketch. Devlin hands him a dime.

The map turns out to be quite accurate. There are only a few turns. They can see some other paths that lead to other hunting camps, but only one of the paths has fresh wagon tracks. It's been just ninety minutes since they arrived in town, but their search has been quite fruitful. Devlin and his men draw their guns and close in on Amanda's campsite.

# Chapter 50

## *The Cover of Night*

One nice thing about living in a quiet and remote camp is that a camper can pick up on every nuance and change in the woods. This is especially true when the camper has been living in the wild for several days.

When the intruders are still a half mile away, Amanda hears a change in the pattern of the bird calls. Some birds grow quieter. Others grow louder. Several birds scatter ahead of the riders, sounding their alarms.

When the riders are over fifteen hundred feet away, she hears twigs breaking and the low rumble of horse hooves.

"I don't believe it," she mutters. "Why would anyone be out here now?"

Feeling cautious, she grabs the box and several personal items before slipping away into the woods. She finds a thick fern patch a few hundred feet up a side trail, crawls into the middle of its lush greenness, and feels the blanket of vegetation completely swallow her.

The men see the steam wagon when they arrive, and this gives Devlin a boost of confidence. "We're in the right place, boys!"

But he's enraged when they find the hut empty. He also finds nothing of value in the wagon.

"Spread out!" Devlin shouts. "Every trail in every direction. Search it. Patrol the woods. Follow the edge of the lake!"

Amanda curses herself for not parking the wagon away from the camp and hiding it beneath branches.

Their search goes on for over two hours. Amanda lies perfectly still. At one point, they venture within 50 feet from her.

Despite all their looking, they find nothing. "Fuck it!" one of the men shouts. "She ain't here. I say we take what we can and be gone."

Devlin hasn't told the others about the jewels he is chasing, so he creates an excuse for them to go search near the lake again. When they're gone, he reenters the hut. He pulls up every loose board that he can find. He even kicks over the stove and knocks holes in the walls. He goes outside and looks under the hut too. In a final act of anger, he removes what food he can from the cabin then sets fire to the hut. He stands and watches it burn and waits until sparks have fizzled out. By that time, it's dark and growing late.

They make a meager meal out of the food stolen from the cabin, and get to talking about what they should do from here.

"I say we at least take that contraption over there. That must be worth something."

Devlin reluctantly agrees, but says he has no intention of hauling it all the way back to Boston. "Maybe we can sell it along the way."

At first, they try hooking it to their horses, but Amanda filled the water tank before she shut it down and they have little luck pulling the heavy wagon up a short incline.

"Well, why don't we just fire it up? I used to work for the railroad. How hard can it be to figure out how to run the damn thing?"

They gather enough material to start a fire under the boiler. Once it gets going, they shovel in more fuel from the coal bin. As the water heats up, they consume the last of Amanda's food.

It's nearly dawn by the time they walk down to the pond to fill their canteens, and the wagon has built up a good head of steam.

In the dim, early light, Amanda hears them laughing and cursing down by the water, so she sticks her head out. She counts them. One… two… three. Yes, that's all of them down there by the water, a good 400 yards away. Amanda slowly emerges from her hiding place, staying low so as not to be seen. She quickly unties the men's horses and reties them to the back of the wagon, then she slips into the driver's spot.

With a quick yank, she forces the steam engine into gear. There's a loud, groaning *thunk,* and it lurches forward. Wheels spinning, it starts to climb the short hill that leads out of the camp.

"What? Hey!" She hears from below. The men try to run up the hill too. With the wheels spinning, Amanda worries they might catch her. But once the wagon starts to bite, it moves faster and the runners are no match for it. With horses in tow, she pulls out of the camp's narrow path and onto a larger dirt road.

One of the men pulls his gun and fires once, twice, three times. The first two shots go wide, but the third whizzes past Amanda and strikes the wagon's boiler tank near its top seam. Scalding steam shoots out of the hole and hisses like a tea kettle. It's a small hole and it won't stop her, but the pressure in the tank will suffer.

Straightening the wagon's direction after her turn, Amanda accelerates as fast as she can.

"You hit her?" Devlin demands as the wagon disappears.

"No, I missed her, God damn it. But I think I hit the cart. I saw some steam shoot up."

"Well, I underestimated her," Devlin mutters. "She got the horses too. Now how are we going to catch her?"

Up the road, the tied horses gallop hard to keep up with the rushing cart. Using her free hand, Amanda throws several handfuls of coals into the firebox. If she keeps the boiler hot, maybe it won't matter that some of the steam is escaping through the bullet hole.

# Chapter 51

## *Where You Ought to Be*


Amanda decides she can't go back into the town. That's the first place the men will head if they're walking. Instead, she drives farther north. The morning sun rises to her right.

She picks her way through dirt roads, and by late morning, she emerges into a rural area south of Concord.

She doesn't want to leave a trail of witnesses behind, so she avoids the downtown area and specifically selects roads where she can see for at least a half mile. If she notices someone walking or riding in the road, she backs up and selects another road before anyone can identify her or the vehicle she is driving.

Eventually she makes her way north of the state's capital city.

She encounters more hills, and the power coming from the wagon starts to wane. Steam shoots from the hole. She needs to find a place that can repair the tank, and that means taking the risk of being noticed by some of the locals.

Reluctantly, Amanda pulls onto a more populated road and heads toward a group of white buildings she sees in the distance. Because of her diminishing steam and speed, it takes her nearly ten minutes to reach the place.

As she coasts into a wide arcing driveway, she is greeted with a puzzling scene. She's not sure what this place is. There's a big square house, a beautiful white church, and several large barns. There are also three complexes of attached buildings stretching to the north, south, and east. In some ways, this looks like a typical New England village, yet there are no standalone homes. The focal point is the big house and barns, while the other buildings appear to be dormitories set up for communal living.

Past the buildings, she sees a series of drainage ditches leading away from the village and across some fields. It appears the fields used to be marshlands. The drainage network helped convert the swamp into rich dark farmlands. But that work must have been completed

173

sometime in the past. It does not look like any crops were planted this year.

Beyond the fields is a hill cleared of most trees and scraped flat on its top. Tall eastern pine trees have been planted along the edges of the flat area, essentially creating what looks like a big outdoor room.

"And who might *ye* be?" a voice calls from her right. The voice startles Amanda because the man literally has to shout to be heard over the noise of the engine.

He looks like a farmer and carries a long wooden pitchfork. Amanda worries she has interrupted his chores. The stranger wears dark pants and a gray woolen shirt that's far too large for him. He looks more like a medieval peasant than a typical farmer.

"I… um… I'm looking for someone who can repair some metal," Amanda replies.

"Well, we used to have someone who could. But we don't no more. Used to be right a'forn that barn."

Amanda sees a small building with a large outdoor coal pit and some metal anvils.

The man walks around the engine, looking it up and down. "I can tell you where another blacksmith is though. About three miles 'o here. Up this same road, then down the hill and second barn to the left."

He reaches out to touch the engine but pulls his hand out when he feels the heat. "But first, can ye tell me? What is this contraption? Looks to be a train, but what's happened here? Has it done run off its tracks?"

Amanda nods. "I guess that's about as good an explanation as any. I can steer the front wheels though, so I don't need tracks."

The man shakes his head in amazement. "God's creatures come to us in many different ways. But can't say as I've seen anyone come in like this 'afor."

Amanda looks toward the white buildings. "Where is 'here' exactly?"

"Here? Why here is where people *ought* to be. That's what we say. It's not up to me to question anyone's choices. But here is the very best place there is in God's world. The only real place." His words come out almost like a song.

Amanda still feels confused. She also remains concerned about the escaping steam. The longer she lingers, the harder it will be to get the cart moving again.

"So, I'll ask ye again," the man says. "Who might ye be?"

She thinks his dialect is as strange as his clothing. "My name is Amanda," she says tentatively.

"Ah yes, from the Latin," he smiles. "Meaning love, or worthy of love."

Amanda grins at this. "Is that true? Well, I'd like to think so."

"So, you don't know where ye are then, eh, dear?"

"Frankly, I haven't the foggiest notion," she says.

"Well," the man tells her with obvious pride, "we are the followers of Mother Ann Lee. This here is her community. We are part of the United Society of Believers."

She looks at him blankly.

"You may know us as the Shaking Quakers."

Amanda has heard the name before, and she searches her mind for a distant memory. The Shakers. She has heard of them. Believers in communal living. Builders of furniture. And baskets and wooden boxes. Singers of hymns.

She remembers more. Men and women work side by side, but lead separate lives. There is no touching. No sex. No children. It's a community based on spirituality that eschews the traditional family structure.

"I see" is all she manages by way of response.

As she talks with the man, a Shaker woman strolls up the driveway. At first, she seems fearful of the hissing cart, but she draws closer when she notices Amanda.

"You appear to be a woman in a hurry. Perhaps even a woman in trouble," says the farmer. "Surely you can see, dear, that what steered you here is God's good providence."

He nods toward the hissing tank, adding, "And if I'm not mistaken, that hole looks to be the result of a bullet? Yes?"

The woman now stands directly next to the man and pulls her white shawl tight over her black dress.

175

"It is," Amanda sighs. And, yes, you could say that I'm in a bit of a hurry. That's why I really need to get to the blacksmith's shop."

The Shaker woman holds up a hand, as if to silence Amanda. "All who enter here are kept safe by the graces of God. And while only God can promise and deliver absolute sanctuary, you are welcome to stay at this place as long as you may want." She points to one of the dormitory buildings. "We have plenty of space, good food, and plenty of work."

The man nods. "Work is a form of worship, you know. We live simply, and quite happily. All who are willing to work can stay for a time and see if this be their true calling."

Amanda stares. Happiness. Safety. Community. Even a purpose. Some of what they describe does seem enticing. But she's already had enough regimented structure in her life. She's worried this would be yet another overbearing and unforgiving place.

"Men and women are equal here," she hears those words as the man continues his lecture. "Do you know that? No differences in the eyes of the Lord. We are all his humble servants."

Amanda tugs at one of the levers. "Please. I need to get this thing fixed before I lose my remaining steam. Can you please just point me to the road that leads to the blacksmith's shop?"

The man looks a bit disappointed. "Promise you'll think about returning? Maybe pay us a longer visit?"

"Yes, yes, certainly."

He reluctantly repeats details on the route that will take her to the shop. She thanks him with a wave and slowly putters away.

# Chapter 52

## *Bars*

The guard appears at the door of Jeb's cell. Mid-thirties, Jeb supposes. Thin mustache. Bit of a belly that makes his footsteps fall a bit harder.

It's an hour past sunset. Jeb knows the watchman has not come to coordinate a release. He looks at the guard, then looks away.

This same man in blue already has appeared twice at Jeb's door. He doesn't come to unlock. He doesn't' directly threaten. He just leans close enough to whisper, and he uses those whispers to taunt. And to laugh.

"So, they're going to take you to see Judge Henry. I just found that out, Jeb. Ain't that great? Old Henry. Oh, that judge does love the police. He loves us guards too. He takes care of us. So, you know what, Jeb? It's always a good thing for us when a case we're interested in goes to old Judge Henry. Know what I mean there, boy?"

Jeb doesn't engage.

The guard bangs his club on the bars. "What's the matter? Can't you speak? Ain't you got any brains there, boy? Let me remind you, you killed yourself a cop. Got caught carrying his gun, didn't you, ya fool. And here you are now, being watched. Watched by another officer. What the hell did you think would happen? You're just damn lucky no one has stepped in there to knock you senseless yet. But you just think about that. Could still happen, right? Middle of the night maybe? You won't know it's coming. So, you just think about that, boy, and you think about it all night and day, you damn yellow lowlife. I want you to keep thinking about it."

"I didn't kill any policeman. I didn't steal the gun."

"Yeah, yeah. Tell it to the judge."

The taunting goes on for several more minutes. Then the guard leaves. His heavy footsteps echo down the granite corridor of the massive Charles Street Jail. With over 200 cells to watch, the guard will be gone for a while. But Jeb knows he'll be back. He undeniably enjoys the bullying.

177

Jeb rises from his cot and walks to his tiny barred window. In the distance, he can see moonlight. And in that moonlight, he pictures the face of Amanda. He sees the shape of her nose. The curve of her cheek. He remembers the smell and the flow of her hair, including that strand near her forehead that never seemed to stay in place.

Then he pictures her the last time he saw her. Piloting that absurd steam wagon away from their attempted ambush. She tried to hit Devlin. Almost succeeded. Jeb knows she would have run him down too, if she had the chance.

He tries to force that thought away from his mind. Instead, he pictures her as a friendly face. He pictures their better times, like their travels to the west. The loving moments they spent on the train, and their first days in Montana.

But every memory of her dissolves back here, to these bars and these granite blocks. She is gone to him. Gone for good this time. And now he's here.

He squints his eyes, lowers his head, and waits for the return of the mocking guard.

# Chapter 53

## *A Fair Exchange*

Amanda finds the blacksmith shop and tries to be at least partially honest when talking to the big man in the leather apron.

"Some men were chasing me," she explains. "I think they... um... wanted to steal this wagon."

She climbs down and gives her usual explanation about what the big cart is, how it works, and how she came to possess it. Then she points to the bullet hole. "Is this something that you can fix?"

The smith puts on a heavy leather glove that lets him touch the hot surface of the metal tank.

"Well, not by welding or pouring new iron. Ain't got the right equipment for that. But I can plug her up with a fat bolt, pour some lead over it and then rivet a metal patch over the top. That should get you back to about 90 percent of the pressure she could handle before. But if I do that, just don't go to full heat again. It might melt the lead."

"Yes, yes. That will do fine. I don't actually have money to pay you though."

She sees him look at her suspiciously, so she quickly adds, "But perhaps you'd be willing to take one of these fine horses in trade?"

The blacksmith looks surprised. "Well, I don't know. Maybe. I have to ask you though, are them horses stolen, ma'am?"

She decides to level with him. At least partially. She makes no mention of the box or the diamonds and instead places the focus on the steam wagon.

"Look, when those men came to steal this cart, I managed to escape when they were away from their horses. I took the horses with me so they couldn't follow. It was the only thing I could think of. But that was miles from here."

She gives him her best smile. The one, as a woman, that she knows usually works on men. "I don't think they have any idea which way I ran."

He looks carefully at the nicest horse. "It's a fine one, all right. But if you're lying to me...."

179

"I'm just telling you how I got here. You can see the bullet hole. When someone tries to attack me, their horses are fair game, I'd say."

As they talk, the smith's dog wanders over. Sniffing Amanda's hand, he wags his tail and nudges her, looking for a pat.

"What a wonderful dog. Retriever?"

"Ayah. Well, mostly. About four years old, and still feisty as hell. Name's Zeke. He don't usually warm up to people too quick. So, he must like you."

"Well," Amanda says as she strokes the dog's head, "I've had animals of one type or another my whole life. Maybe he can tell."

When the dog gets too pesky with its nudges, the blacksmith shoos him away. "Come on, Zeke! Back inside." After the dog is gone, the smith offers a deal.

"Look, I'll go ahead and do the work in trade for the horse. Don't know if that's really the right thing to do or not, but it ain't obvious to me that it's the wrong thing either. Plus, my dog thinks you're a nice person, and I can always use a horse."

"Thank you," Amanda smiles. "Do you have any idea how long...?"

"It's going to take me the rest of the day to fix it, so you'd best find yourself something to do."

With that, he releases the steam, uses a bucket to drown the fire, and lets the cart cool.

"While we're waiting," he says, "let's see what we can do to strengthen that wobbling wheel."

Amanda hadn't even noticed.

# Chapter 54

## Hard Ride

Devlin and his hired men stay together. Since they lack horses, they walk until they spot a barn with an outdoor corral. There they spot a few stout mounts. They see no one nearby. Devlin scoops some hay from the ground and ducks under a fence rail. It only takes a few minutes to win the trust of three of the animals.

They'll have to ride bareback, but they can make it work.

The stolen mounts turn out to be good strong horses, but they're not built for speed. They're working stock.

A mile away, they pull up and make their plans.

"The way I figure it," Devlin says, "that girl didn't go back into town. I could hear that damn engine chugging for a while, and it wasn't headed that direction. Ain't that what you figure, Earl?"

Earl, the man in the gray hat, nods. "If she didn't go into town, then she definitely has to be headed this direction. No other real road out here." He points northwest. "I been near here before when I was a kid. Ain't much at all in that direction until you get to the hills. Spread your arc out a little wider, you still ain't going to hit more than four villages."

The other man, whose name is Pruitt, shakes his head. "I don't see us catching up. Too many places to look."

But Devlin says he likes the odds. "When you got a small town, you ain't got more than a place or two in each that's capable of fixing a hole in a boiler. All right then, if we split up, we should be able to check most of them within the next day."

Pruitt shakes his head again. "That's a hell of a lot of riding. And we've done a lot already. I don't like the odds at all. And I ain't seen any money yet."

"The hell with the odds," Devlin shouts and points his finger for emphasis. "We're going to find her because we're going to outwork her. We know her direction. We know what she needs to get fixed. Hell, this should be easy. We've just got to move fast."

In his mind, Devlin pictures a box full of diamonds. To him, that's the prize that should make this whole effort worthwhile.

"Yeah, well, I think I'm done with this wild-goose chase," says Pruitt. "Never expected to be riding out this far with you. Never expected to lose my horse. So for pay, I'm right happy with just this new horse. If you just pay me for the past two days, I guess I'll be on my way."

Devlin looks disgusted. "Pay you? I'll pay you when we're done. Not a minute before. If you want to cut out early, then it's your loss."

Pruitt looks to Earl. "You hear that? You on board with that? The man here says he ain't going to pay us."

Earl shrugs. "I figure we signed on and knew it would take time. I'm going to see it through."

Pruitt spits in disgust. "Damn, you two are something else. Riding all over hell. Must be something special that girl has that you ain't telling me about. Or maybe you're sweet on her. Is that it?"

Devlin just gives Pruitt a cold look. "Yeah. That's it. Sweet on her. You got me."

"Well, God damn. Suit yourself, boys. I'm turning back. This is a better horse than I had before, so I figure I'm at least coming out a little bit ahead. And you can just go to hell for holding back on the pay."

He rides away at full gallop, knowing full well a gun could be trained on his back.

"What do we do now, boss?" Earl asks. "There's more territory out there than we can cover with just the two of us."

Devlin yanks the reins and sends his horse in the direction of Amanda's escape. "What do we do? We ride, and we ask questions. And we also try to find a man or two we can hire. Then we have those boys ride down the side roads. We tell them what to look for. We do what we have to do to find her, damn it, and we keep on doing it *until* we find her. That's the commitment."

Earl shrugs, then follows. He's never seen this kind of fire in a man's belly before. If nothing else, it might be interesting to see where this all leads.

# Chapter 55

## *Parts and Places*

Later that afternoon, Amanda unhitches one of her stolen horses and follows the road from the blacksmith's. She reaches a small crossroads that includes a store and a grange hall.

Luck is with her. The store is open.

She looks at the meager offerings, selects some fruit and bread and a woven blanket, chosen because she suspects the coming evening will be surprisingly cool.

She places her choices on the counter. When the clerk arrives, Amanda points to a telegraph machine on a far counter.

"Tell me something, would you be interested in selling me that equipment?"

The man behind the counter laughs. "Whatever for? Do you have your own private telegraph line?"

"No. I just need some of the parts from it."

The shopkeeper scratches his beard. "Well, my first reaction is no. I make a little bit of money from that telegraph once per week or so. But my father started this store, and one of the things he taught me was that 'everything is always for sale.'" He leans over the counter. "So, I guess my answer is, it depends on the price."

Amanda reaches into her purse and selects one of the smaller diamonds. "Well, I could offer this, but the deal is that you'd also need to let me borrow a wagon for a couple days to deliver it. Think we could make a deal?"

The man's eyes widen. He takes the stone and walks to his front window where he examines its facets in the waning sunlight. He finds a magnifying glass and gives it an even closer inspection. Eventually he grins and calls out to her.

"You want to take that equipment right now? Or do you want it tomorrow?

"I'll pick it up later," Amanda replies. "But I need a bit of information first. I'm looking for either a power plant or a factory that uses electricity, maybe one that has its own generators?"

The store owner thinks about this for a while. "We really ain't got much of that sort of thing around here. Not at all."

"Can you think though? There must be something, somewhere. Where have you seen electric lights in the windows?"

"Huh. Well, there's a town not far from here… there's a whole complex of mills there, built around the river. I've seen lights there."

"Is there a power company in town?" she asks.

"There's not. So, I imagine the mills must have their own generators."

"Perfect," Amanda smiles. "My horse is outside. Can you help me hook up the wagon and give me some directions?"

She rides to the outskirts of town and parks the wagon behind an abandoned barn. Sleeping in the bed of the wagon isn't very comfortable, but it's not terrible, considering some of the places she slept in recent weeks. She ends up sleeping curled up like a ball, to ward off the cold.

At first light, she rides to the mill complex and tries the doors until she finds one that's open.

Inside, workers stare at her, dumbfounded. Amanda demands to see the shop foreman.

The foreman, who turns out to be the son of the owner, looks angry when he appears, and obviously intends to show Amanda to the door. But a small diamond again works like a charm. Actually, it takes two diamonds in this case.

"No, I can't sell you a generator," he insists at first. But he's young. Amanda discovers she has exactly what he needs because he's engaged to be married.

With two diamonds in hand, he gives her the plant's smallest generator and helps load it into the wagon.

Amanda returns to the store by early afternoon. As the shopkeeper carries the telegraph equipment outside, he looks at the generator with great surprise.

"What in the world are you doing with all this stuff, ma'am?" he inquires.

"Just starting a new hobby," Amanda smiles.

"Well, I don't know what you're really plotting. But it certainly does seem like you have some kind of a plan."

She drives the wagon, full of equipment, back to the blacksmith's shop and sees that her steam wagon has been repaired. Tugging at the horse leads, she expertly backs the wagon up, stopping it near the rear of the steam wagon. The blacksmith claps when he sees her skills.

With his help, she pushes the small generator into the bed of the steam wagon and also transfers the telegraph parts and several lengths of wire.

By the time she returns the wagon to the store and returns, the blacksmith has filled the water tank and started a fire under it.

Amanda scans the horizon. "Tell me, do you know what the tallest point is around here? At least a tall point that has a road that goes all the way to the top?"

"How far away do you want to go? Here in town, we have a couple good-sized hills about four miles apart maybe."

"I'm looking for the highest point in the whole state."

He laughs. "Well, there's little doubt about that." He points to a hazy bump on the horizon. "That's Mount Washington, highest point in all of the Northeast."

Amanda asks how to get there.

The blacksmith gives her directions. "I know it has some kind of road. They put it in years ago. Started out as a logging trail, then they extended it all the way to attract visitors and carriages."

She nods.

"Long ride from here though. Mind telling me what you're really doing?"

She smiles, "Let's just say I'm trying to return something that doesn't belong to me."

She points to the horses, "Can you watch them for a few days? Then you can pick the one you want to keep."

"Of course. I'd be happy to."

When the cart reaches full steam, she pulls away, heading northwest as the sun sinks low.

# Chapter 56

## *A Different Path*

"Good morning," says a man on a horse whose face is not quite visible.

The blacksmith, hard at work, grunts a hello.

Even though the visitor has a dust cloth covering his mouth and nose, the smithy can tell the man is very tired. He suspects he's been riding all night.

"I understand you may have a piece of my property," the man on the horse says.

The smith wipes his hands on an oily cloth. "That so?"

Just then Zeke the dog wanders out of the barn and starts to bark. The man with the hidden face backs up a bit on his horse, hand sliding down toward his belt.

"What kind of property are you missing, and how might it have ended up here?"

"It's a wagon. A steam wagon. Believe it was driven in by a woman."

"I see. And who are you?"

Devlin Richards lies from beneath his face cover. "Name's... umm... Colby."

Zeke trots over to stand by the blacksmith's side. He offers another low growl as a second man rides up to join Devlin.

"Colby, huh?"

Devlin nods.

"That's funny. Because I heard your name was Richards or something like that."

Behind Devlin, Earl grows impatient, "I guess that answers our question about whether that whore has been here."

The blacksmith ignores the comment and looks over at their mounts. "That's a strong-looking horse you're riding there, Mr. Colby, or Mr. Richards, or whatever the hell your name is." He points toward the hooves. "Fact, he looks a bit like a plow horse."

"Yes, well, times are tough, and a good, strong horse is a good, strong horse. I like riding this one. You have a problem with that?"

"Well, as a matter of fact, I do. You see, in my business, I see a lot of horses. Especially working horses. I know this horse. I can even see that he's wearing my shoes. That there is a stallion belongs to Earnest Miller. Lives about eight miles from here."

Devlin stares at him for a moment. "You are very astute, sir. It is indeed Mr. Miller's horse. I bought the animal from him this morning."

"That a fact? You have a receipt?"

"I do. But that's no damn business of yours. I'm here to collect my property."

"If you intend to continue talking with me, then I intend to make that receipt part of my business. Got it? You get nothing until I see it."

"Step back, Devlin," the other rider hisses. His hand goes into his coat. The dog growls again.

Devlin holds up his hand, delaying his friend.

"Okay, since you seem to want to know, we actually borrowed these horses. We're trying to catch up with a woman who stole ours. Fact is, she stole that special wagon from us too. If we get everything back, we will gladly leave these horses right here, and they can be safely returned to Farmer Miller."

The blacksmith squints. "You know, don't ya, that a man can still get hanged for stealing horses?"

"How about a woman?" Earl replies.

The blacksmith folds his arms across his chest. He stands firm, like a grimy Greek statue.

Several silent moments pass. Zeke growls again and leans against his owner's leg.

"Look, we're wasting time. Where did the woman go?"

"I don't know."

"The hell you don't!" Devlin sneers. "Tell me something, mister, did you see a box?"

The blacksmith frowns.

"Yeah. A box. How'd she pay you? She's snookered you, mister. And we need to catch up. You'll thank us."

The blacksmith considers this turn of events. He doesn't want to mention he bargained for one of the horses hidden in his barn. He delivers his response in carefully measured tones.

"I'll tell you what. You go file a report with the local police. Okay? I'll even ride up to the town hall with you. You file a report. You let the police sort it out, and then I'll be happy to help you find your wagon *and* your horses."

He smiles in satisfaction, but in a flash, he finds himself staring down the barrel of a gun.

"You want to meet your maker there, smithy?"

The blacksmith holds his hands up. "No need for..."

"Then you tell us. Now."

"Okay, okay. Just lower the gun. She went to the train station," he lies. "Said she was going to take a train west. May not have left yet."

Zeke continues to growl. Devlin's horse looks at the dog and shifts uneasily, just enough to slightly move Devlin's arm and the gun. Realizing he's out of the direct line of fire for a moment, the blacksmith bolts to the left. Zeke nips at the horse's heels.

Wheeling around as the horse rears up, Devlin expertly forces his mount to settle down and face front again. He fires at the running blacksmith, hitting him square in the back as he reaches the door of his shop. The big man stumbles and falls, nearly out of sight. Devlin's horse rears up again, but he stays in control. Zeke runs over to his master and stands nearby, whining and licking his face.

Devlin and Earl circle the shop a few times. Eventually they find tracks and realize the cart exited on a small rear path.

"Train station, my ass."

The path cuts diagonally across the field, taking Amanda in a whole new direction. They follow the path over the field, then through a small valley and a stand of tall pines.

"She came out right here, see? Turned north."

They follow her trail until dark. Devlin holds a match low, illuminating a small circle of dusty road. The prints from the big wooden wheels are unmistakable, but he struggles to follow them at night.

"Where do you think she's headed?" Earl asks.

"Doesn't look like she has much of a plan." Devlin stares down the road. "She's just running. Heading into nothing but mountains. Best guess is that she'll stop at the next town, whatever the hell it is. She knows she needs to lay low someplace."

He doesn't share his true concern with Earl—that Amanda could have hidden the box and the diamonds anywhere along the way. If that's the case, he'll need to make her talk, and it won't be pleasant. Not for him or her.

"Wherever she stops, we're going to find her." Devlin strokes his scar and jabs his heels into his horse, lurching on down the road and into the darkness.

# Chapter 57

## *Splice*


Victor can't help but think about Amanda. He mulls her words over in his mind. Reading her diary definitely has piqued his curiosity. If only he knew how to contact her.

His crew received a huge load of materials that morning and Victor has fully resumed supervising the installations. They have enough to add 20 more miles of wires and insulators. To accomplish this, they fall into a dull routine. He watches as they attach new wires to new wooden poles, and every few poles, he climbs up to inspect how they've secured both the wires and the insulators.

Every thousand feet or so, they empty a large spool, and that means they have to splice in the wires from a new spool.

That's usually when he has the time to climb up a pole, and tap into the electricity. As he has done so many times, he holds his antenna and listens for the spark generated by Professor Alton. But the spark is almost undetectable at this distance.

One of his workers shouts up to him. "Still playing with your toys, boss?"

"You know it. So, you know I've been picking up a signal from Boston, right? Well, it's almost gone now."

The man nods. "Maybe I should learn more about this radio stuff. This linemen work isn't going to last forever. Might need some other way to make a living."

Victor laughs. "Well, I wouldn't discourage you. Radio could be a big thing very soon. But..."

He gestures down the road and toward the hills beyond, "I can tell you that wires aren't going away either. Even just doing what you're doing now, you will have more than enough work to last your lifetime."

# Chapter 58

## *View from the Top*

Amanda rubs her eyes. She drove through the night and only made one stop for water and coal. She makes one additional stop, as close to the mountain as possible. She purchases some fuel and oil for the generator, plus enough food to last five days.

When she reaches the base of Mount Washington, she is stunned by how high it is. This doesn't belong in New England. This belongs out in the West, like the mountains she saw so many weeks ago. It's immense and steep and jagged. She drives along the base for quite a while, until she finds the road that leads to the summit. Her biggest worry right now is the wear and tear on the old cart. Even with Jonathan and Jasper's repairs, even with the help of that nice blacksmith, this cart was never meant to be pushed the way she has been pushing it. Its wheels are starting to wobble again. The levers seem to grind like sandpaper. But she presses on and wonders if the cart will ever come down again after making this climb.

The steam engine works extra had to force its way up the steep incline. In spite of the cart's other problems, the engine itself is as strong as ever. It does its job of putting power to the wheels. It takes nearly two hours, with the cart slowly losing its power along the way, but she finally reaches the top of the mountain. The view is incredible. Sun and clouds and a vast stretch of fall colors. There's a small tourist hut to her left. There are posters in the windows advertising candy and beer, but a hand-written sign on the front door says the hut is closed for the season. That's fine with her. More privacy.

Amanda pulls the steam car onto a flat area, then turns her attention to a far different kind of engine – the generator in the back.

Pulling out Victor's diary, she looks at the sketches, including the recent ones made by Tesla.

Amanda starts stringing wires and fastening bolts, stopping often to examine the drawings. Once everything is properly wired, she walks around and finds three sticks. She lashes them into a simple tripod. On top of this, she places the coil that Jasper found inside the puzzle box.

She then attaches the last few wires. They link to special bolts on the sides of the coil. The arrangement reminds her of a sawed-off coffee can being consumed by vines.

"How anyone ever figured out this electrical stuff is beyond me," she mumbles. But she rechecks the connections and confirms she has followed the diagram.

In her mind, she runs through the instructions she received when she bought the generator. Fuel goes here. Check the oil. Engine is at the back. The engine powers the generator via a short leather belt. The electricity comes from there. Use the crank to start the engine. Let the engine run for a minute, then engage the generator.

Check, check, and… check.

It takes her eight tries to get the engine started, but once she does, it whirs to life. Then she engages the belt, and the generator portion starts humming.

Electricity immediately starts flowing to the coil, which also starts to hum.

A second set of wires comes back from the coil, to the magnet and switch of the telegraph key. The coil sparks with an even tap-tap-tap sound. She can use the telegraph key to manipulate the length of the spark, sometimes short, sometimes long. Sometimes a second or two with no spark.

She sets the telegraph key on top of the wagon and begins tapping. She does four simple dots, then waits. That's what the man who sold her the telegraph suggested. She hopes this will mean "hello" to anyone who detects the signal.

Taking a seat beside the key, she again taps four dots, then stops. She repeats the pattern for over an hour, until her hand grows tired.

Pulling some apples and bread from her sack, she decides to take a break.

Amanda will try to send her signal again in an hour. She will keep trying, every hour or two, for the next couple of days.

"Or at least until my hand goes numb."

In between, she studies a Morse code card that came with the telegraph. When she is through studying, she looks out over the broad valleys. "I don't know if you're listening, Victor, but I'm trying to do this. I don't know that it will work, but if anyone can pick up this signal, it's you."

# Chapter 59

## *Methodical*

"Damn gravel roads," Devlin says with disgust.

They had been able to track Amanda for several miles, thanks to the ruts left in the dirt. But when they reach a gravel road at sun-up, those ruts disappear. The problem is compounded by the fact that crossroads exist every few miles, and some of them are gravel too. She could have pulled onto any of them. This puts two trackers in a situation where they have to explore each crossroad, following it for several hundred yards and looking for evidence of ruts.

"Tedious work," Earl laments. "And my ass is damn sore from sitting on this horse."

"We've come this far," says Devlin. "Can't quit it now."

"I ain't saying I'm quitting it," Earl says. "I'm just grousing is all. I said I'd be in it for the full haul. Let's keep going."

Devlin nods. "I appreciate it. You go that way, I'll go this. One of us spots something, we ride to find the other, and then we go on."

As Earl follows one of the roads, Devlin pats the gun in his coat pocket. It's a new gun he bought in Boston after losing the police pistol.

In some ways, he's going to hate using the gun on Earl. The man's turned out to be one of the better partners he's ever had for this kind of work. Earl may be a Yankee, but he would have made a damn good Rebel, Devlin decides. Strong. Reliable. Earl is the sort of man who is honest with his partners and ruthless to others.

Yes, it will be a damn shame to kill him. But diamonds make everything different.

Once Devlin recovers them, he's not going to share. That was the plan from the beginning. Come north, take all the riches he can, and don't let anyone get in his way.

# Chapter 60

## *Out of the Noise*

Victor squints at the gauge on his receiver as he stands atop a New Hampshire power pole. Something strange is happening. Besides the weak signal he's receiving from Professor Alton, he sees a second signal of some sort. In fact, this other signal seems stronger, as if its origin is closer to him than the professor's tower that's located many miles to the south.

Whenever this other signal appears, it clicks much louder and clearer.

He spins the antenna on its axis and focuses on just the new signal. It's a simple repeating pattern. Four dots.

Unable to figure out what's going on, he pulls the four-foot antenna bar from its mount on top of the electrical pole and holds it sideways. The direction of a signal can be determined by swinging an antenna in a 360-degree circle. Reception is the strongest when the long flat side of his antenna is facing the direction of the signal.

To Victor's utter surprise, he discovers the second signal is not coming from Boston. Instead, it's coming from somewhere north of him. *This must be a mistake. There's no possible radio source in that direction.*

Victor checks and rechecks his readings. Then the signal stops. Shaking his head, he returns to his work. But he checks several more times over the course of the day. The signal appears again two hours later. He listens for a long time and discovers the new signal stops and starts, at perfect half-hour intervals. But all he sees in that direction are big hills. Very big.

He works through the day with his wire crew. When he has spare moments, he tries to figure out what might be causing the radio waves. He's stymied and eventually he grows tired.

But that night in his tent, a flash of insight comes. Victor sits bolt upright in his bed. Who else, in all of New England, would have a coil capable of sending a radio signal? Besides the professor, there's only one spark generator he can think of.

It's the one he lost. It's the one he now knows has been found.

"It has to be her!" he says aloud. "Who else could it be? Amanda – the one who sent me her diary! I know she has it. But… actually getting it to work? How?"

The diary he received from her didn't contain much, but he read enough to know she seems intelligent and driven. And since she also read his journal, she might get a rudimentary idea of how the coil works. But how could anyone be smart enough to piece together a fully powered radio transmitter when all she started with was his basic coil? Why would she even try?

The next morning, he sets up the receiver and battery again, and once again, every half hour, the dots start repeating. As he predicts, a half hour later, they stop.

The next time he detects the transmission, he confirms that it's coming from the northern mountains. Maybe even the tallest one. He also realizes the signal now is longer than just four dots. Sometimes other dots and dashes are mixed in, as if the sender of the signal has grown bored with the four-dot pattern.

When the different pattern starts, he writes down the Morse code letters. What he sees makes him smile.

A M A N D A

And then the signal returns to just the four dots.

Victor grins a wild, crazy grin. *Oh my God,* he thinks to himself. *It can't be.* But it is. It's definitely her. She's learned basic Morse code. She is saying hello and occasionally typing her own name, just for fun.

Victor looks toward the mountains. All right, if he was going to try to send a signal to the world, he might have selected a tall mountain too. Maybe the tallest one. Why not? He can see the peak of Mount Washington. *There's even a road to the top,* he thinks. *It's been there for years.*

That's a wise woman right there.

If only he could send a message back. His equipment can only receive and hers can only transmit. He can't even warn her the electricity in the coil can sometimes behave in strange and unpredictable ways.

He quickly gives his wire crews some detailed assignments, enough to keep them busy until the weekend. "I have to go back to the central office for some meetings," he lies. "I'll be back in a couple days."

Unhooking a horse from one of the equipment wagons, he grabs the only saddle they have and rides out of the work camp. Once he's out of sight, he doesn't head toward Boston. Instead, he heads north at a full gallop. As he rides into a rolling landscape of orange, red, and yellow leaves, he has no idea what he might find, but he is more than excited to make the journey.

# Chapter 61

## *Arrival*

Devlin is off his horse and pacing the edge of a road.

Is that a recent disturbance in the dirt? He thought so at first. But now he's uncertain. Wagon ruts? He runs a finger along the ground. The base is hard and dry. He just can't tell.

Earl comes up beside him, riding fast.

"Found it," he shouts. "Found her trail again. No doubt about it with those fat heavy wheels. Less than a mile from here. Come see."

"About fucking time," Devlin snorts. "We've been searching for hours."

They ride hard and reach the spot where two roads diverge. The one on the left has a set of tracks that could only have been made by the heavy steam wagon.

"All right then," Devlin nods. "Good job. She definitely did head this way."

They make progress, but it's slow. The rough gravel continues to hamper their tracking. They still have to look for proof of direction whenever they reach a crossroad. Gradually it dawns on Devlin. The main road is going uphill, not back toward civilization. Each time she has a choice, she's choosing the road that goes up – higher and away from everything. He decides they don't need to keep looking on the side roads. She must be heading toward the mountaintop.

"I don't understand this," Earl says. "Where the hell is she going? Hiding out maybe?"

"Could be, could be."

Devlin isn't sure why she's making this trek, but now that he's figured out Amanda's direction, he doesn't need Earl. His hand instinctively brushes the handle of his gun.

A half hour later, they emerge from the tree line onto a series of rocky rises. Devlin can see the obvious route to the summit. But he's waited too long to use his gun. She's likely to hear it now. Slipping out his knife, Devlin slowly closes in behind Earl with plans for a nice, quiet dispatch.

A few miles away, Victor Marius urges his horse off the road and starts to climb the steep bank through the woods. He's been riding for hours, and the horse is tired. But they press on. He sees a clear stream. Fearing water might be scarce on the mountaintop, he lets the horse drink.

He drums his fingers on the stallion's saddle, then rides again when the horse is finished. By traversing the slope through the trees and doubling back and forth only on the steep parts, he'll be able to reach the mountain top much quicker than if he stayed on the road. The horse puffs and groans at the effort.

As they climb, he can make out a small building near the top, but not much else is visible. Could the signal be coming from that hut? He urges the spent horse to continue. He can feel its iron shoes slip and slide on the rocks, but he holds steady and continues the ascent. The day is clear, but a few pancake-like lenticular clouds sit motionless above the crest.

Victor finally reaches the small building, and finds it closed. Riding around the side, he sees nothing at first, then spies a strange-looking wagon with a locomotive-like front end.

Then he sees her.

Sitting on the ground, next to the wagon, is a woman. She's looking at a small book and tapping a telegraph key.

Victor smiles and shakes his head. The engine is noisy. She can't hear him approaching.

He ties his horse to the building and slowly walks in front of her. She is so intent on her work that she doesn't notice his arrival.

"By any chance," he shouts, "is your name Amanda?"

She looks up with a mixture of confusion and surprise. The look is soon replaced by one of wonder.

"This worked?" She nearly squeals as she stands. "This actually worked?"

He nods and walks toward her. "Looks like it did. So, does that mean you are Amanda? I think you are, and I guess the real question is why are you doing..."

"Wait. What about you?" She struggles to find the words. "Are you Victor?"

He laughs and shouts. "I am, indeed."

"I... I just...." She starts to step toward him then stops, hands on her cheeks. Slightly flustered. "Look, I know you don't know me. But... I sort of know you. I found your journal. And all your notes. I read them. And I found this, this thing..." she holds her hands in front as she tries to show the shape of the spark generator. "And it was inside this wooden puzzle box. And I tried to contact... I mean.... oh!"

With that, she runs to him and embraces him tightly.

"It's so good to finally meet you!"

He laughs, in shock. "How did you ever?" But he stops and finds himself returning her hug, caught up in the wonder of the moment.

"Come, look," she says, motioning to the generator. "See? The electricity comes from here. And these wires go to the coil. Remember your drawings? They weren't really complete. But then I met your friend Tesla. Well, listen to this...."

Victor notices the coil has a bit of a blue glow to it. He steps back, pulling her with him. He makes a mental note to shut the rig down as soon as he can, before the electrical buildup increases.

As her enthusiastic description of the equipment continues, they don't notice a man on horseback as he trots around the far side of the hut. But his movement eventually causes Amanda to look up. She recognizes him from when she aimed the steam car at him in Boston. But it's too late to run.

"Well, you're quite the slippery quarry, aren't ya?" Devlin drawls as he circles the pair. His gun is drawn. A chewed matchstick dangles from his lips. "Wasn't sure if I'd ever catch up to you."

Amanda gives him an angry look. "You! You are a heinously persistent man."

Both Amanda and Victor turn to face Devlin. They must continue turning as he keeps circling them. The yellow-and-orange hills pass behind him as he orbits.

"So, who are you?" Victor demands. "What do you want?" He silently curses himself for not bringing any sort of weapon. But when he rode off to find the source of the radio signal, he never expected a confrontation.

Amanda starts to run toward the wagon, eyes on a heavy bar that sits on the back gate. But Devlin fires a shot at her feet.

"You stop right there, girly. I'm happy to plug you where you stand."

Victor steps in front of her protectively. Instinctively.

"I don't know who you are, mister," Devlin shouts, "I have no quarrel with you. Stand aside. The girl knows why I'm here." He waves the gun. "So, tell me, where's that damn box? And you better start talking."

"I don't know," she lies.

Devlin cocks his pistol and points it directly at Victor. "Well, maybe it will improve your memory if I shoot your friend here first, hmm?"

"What? No! No, you can't!" Amanda feels a genuine moment of dread. Not now. Not after all this time. It can't end like this. Not when they've finally met!

"Okay!" Amanda pleads. "Okay! I can tell you where it is."

As Devlin and Amanda talk, Victor looks around. His gaze settles on the coil. It's still energized and humming as the generator cranks away. The blue glow has increased substantially. That's not good. It needs to be shut down immediately.

But then he gets an idea, though he's not sure if it will work. But then he gives a slight grin.

"I'm going to count to three," Devlin shouts. "One—"

"Over there!" Victor interrupts. "On that tripod. See?"

Devlin looks, and his eyes slowly narrow to a slit. "I don't see any damn box over there!"

"It's just the diamonds. Come on, that's what you're looking for, right? She took them out of the box. They're just sitting on that plate thing over there. Go ahead and look. You can even see them reflecting the sky, right?"

Devlin seems skeptical but dismounts and walks toward the coil. He keeps his gun trained on the pair, giving occasional sideways glances at them, and then at the tripod. He does see a bit of a blue sparkle. He's excited at the thought of finally getting near the treasure –

enough so that he doesn't notice the hair on his head as it starts to stand up.

When he's about two paces from the coil, he starts to feel a ticklish charge of electric current on his face. Then, suddenly, a glowing, bluish-white arc stretches out. The dangerous buildup of electricity has found its path to the ground – and that leads right through Devlin's body.

With a tremendous electrical crackle, the bolt strikes Devlin hard in the head, stiffening him. It sounds like the crack of a baseball bat against a hollow tree.

The arc continues with loud snaps and pops for several seconds. His forehead sizzles. His body teeters, then jerks. When he finally falls, his feet leave a burn mark on the ground.

The energy dissipates with a low hiss and Devlin lies still. The smell of burned hair and flesh fills the air. The blue glow has dissipated for now. Victor runs over, kicks away Devlin's pistol then picks it up. But he can see the threat has passed. The tremendous shock did its job. Devlin is gone.

"What happened?" Amanda demands. She runs to grab Victor's arm.

He points toward the coil. "My older design has a flaw. It draws too much power and gets over-energized. To get rid of it, it will ground itself any way it can, including jumping through the air." He places his arm around her shoulder. "I'm so glad you never walked close to it when it was running. That big spark might have jumped out and hit you instead."

Together they disengage the generator and power down the system. Victor examines the steam car, shaking his head in wonder. Amanda explains that it's many years old, and likely doesn't have many miles left. Halfway through the story, she veers off on a tangent about first seeing the wagon on the beach.

And that was when she found the puzzle box.

And that's how this all started.

And then she's off on another story, about how she managed to open the box, and how the journal helped her learn all about him.

Her excitement is effervescent, then she stops in midsentence. "I'm sorry. I'm rambling. So much to tell you," she says. "So many things I want to say."

Victor climbs on his horse and beckons. He grasps her arm, then swings her into place behind him. She holds him tightly around the waist.

With a flick of the reigns, Victor directs the horse down the mountain. "In that case, I'm glad we found each other. Tell me the whole story," he calls back over his shoulder.

"There's so much I'd like to learn."

The Puzzle Box Chronicles is a series, starting with
Book 1
  Wreck of the Gossamer

* * * *

The Story of Amanda, Jeb, Wayne, Victor, Devlin and others continues
in

The Lost, the Found and the Hidden
The Puzzle Box Chronicles: Book 2

Those Who Wander
The Puzzle Box Chronicles: Book 3

Wires and Wings
The Puzzle Box Chronicles: Book 4

North of Angel Falls
The Puzzle Box Chronicles: Book 5

The Beckoning Spark
The Puzzle Box Chronicles: Book 6

Made in United States
Troutdale, OR
06/18/2023